THE
PROPAGANDIST

THE
PROPAGANDIST

CÉCILE DESPRAIRIES

TRANSLATED FROM THE FRENCH BY NATASHA LEHRER

SWIFT PRESS
First published in Great Britain by Swift Press 2025
First published in the United States of America by New Vessel Press 2024
First published in French in 2023 as La Propagandiste

1 3 5 7 9 8 6 4 2

Copyright © 2023 Éditions du Seuil
Translation copyright © 2024 Natasha Lehrer

The right of Cécile Desprairies to be identified as the Author of
this Work has been asserted in accordance with the Copyright, Designs
and Patents Act 1988.

This work received support for excellence in publication and translation
from AlbertineTranslation, a program of Albertine Foundation in
partnership with Villa Albertine.

Printed and bound in Great Britain by
CPI Group (UK) Ltd, Croydon CR0 4YY

A CIP catalogue record for this book is available from the British Library

We make every effort to make sure our products are safe for the purpose
for which they are intended. Our authorised representative in the EU for product
safety is Easy Access System Europe, Mustamäe tee 50,
10621 Tallinn, Estonia gpsr.requests@easproject.com

ISBN: 9781800755239
eISBN: 9781800755246

To Jeanne

1

When I was a child, I would listen to my mother talking softly to herself about "the 1940s." At the wheel of her gray Citroën 2CV convertible, driving at a steady twenty miles an hour, oblivious to the still-blinking turn signal, she muttered away, at constant risk of an accident. "I didn't see him," would have been her sole excuse.

This was Paris in the mid-1960s. I was six or seven years old, and pretty sure my mother was truly herself only when she was in the car talking to herself, nodding her head with a deep sigh, lifting a beringed hand, then listlessly letting it drop back down to the steering wheel. I sensed, in her long-suffering brooding over the past, an obsession with something I couldn't understand. I thought she must be brave simply to carry on living.

While she waited for the traffic light to change, she fumbled in the glove compartment among a mess of half-melted chocolate-coated caramels, used-up tubes of lipstick, a fake tortoiseshell comb, a headscarf, hairpins, and parking passes to be displayed in the windshield. She checked in the rearview mirror that her face wasn't betraying her and fiddled with her chignon. At such moments, she looked almost at peace.

Sitting in the back seat, reminding her now and then of her responsibilities ("Signal!" "Shift into second gear," "Watch out!"), I listened to her murmuring intensely, over and over, "The bastards!" In response to my prodding, I was told this term referred to all those who had "condemned" Pétain and Laval and "murdered" Henriot. She swallowed the syllables as she uttered their names. I supposed the men had died tragically or perhaps had been victims of a miscarriage of justice. I thought she must be talking about the great-uncles. There were several in the family.

Inside her rattletrap of a car (which she told me was, like a Faraday cage, there to protect us from being struck by lightning), adrift in her musings, and barely responsive, she gave only the vaguest answers to my questions. We were often on our way to the Bois de Boulogne, not far from where we lived, where she was particularly fond of taking me. She told me about the famous restaurant called La Grande Cascade and said we would go there for dinner one day. (I hadn't made any such request.)

"To the restaurant?"

"Yes, we'll go together."

But later, when I reminded her, she insisted I was mistaken.

"I can't have said that. You don't take children to that kind of restaurant."

We stopped at a tall impressive tree known as the "oak of the executed," on which was nailed a rusty plaque with the inscription "Passersby / Respect this oak tree / It bears the traces of the bullets that killed our martyrs." What martyrs? Christian martyrs? My mother's response was cagey.

We headed for the Jardins de Bagatelle. Its name was another mystery. What bagatelle? If it was really some trifling thing, as the name indicated, where was the frivolity, if around the park the talk was all of martyrs?

It was back home in our apartment that I mainly heard talk of "the bastards," when my immediate female relatives—my mother, aunt, cousin, and grandmother—gathered most mornings in an atmosphere that resembled a gynaeceum, the women's quarters in a house in ancient Greece.

We lived in Paris's 17th arrondissement, a not particularly fashionable neighborhood bordering the suburb of Levallois, in a low-rise building that looked onto a garden enclosed by two more buildings, one to the left and one to the right. In the central block, on the second floor, lived my parents, my two brothers, my sister, and me. On the seventh floor of the block on the right, with a view straight into ours, lived my widowed maternal grandmother. After her death, my aunt Zizi, my mother's sister, inherited the apartment. On the third floor of the block on the left lived Zizi's daughter, my cousin Hedy.

This meant that everyone just had to look out of the window to see who was at home. The women watched for the lights to change in our apartment, waiting until the coast was clear; as soon as they were sure my father had left for work, they were at the front door within minutes, practically on his heels, having made every effort to avoid bumping into him. If, despite taking precautions, one of the ladies crossed his path, she murmured an embarrassed "Good morning, Charles," and an awkward pretext to explain what she was doing there so early: "I was just dropping something off for Lucie."

When she was with these women, my mother played down her life as a traditional housewife with a husband and children. Grandmother Hermine, whom I called Herminette, had always kept her life separate from that of her husband and, though they shared an apartment, each had their own bedroom. Widowed relatively young, freed of a husband who had turned out to be more than a little parsimonious but now had the distinct advantage of being deceased, Herminette carried on with her life, grateful at last to be able to spend a little money.

My aunt Denise detested her given name and always called herself Zizi. She too had once had a husband, but a few years after the birth of their daughter they had gotten divorced. She kept her private life shrouded in mystery, now and again alluding to a "friend" whose sex she did not specify and with whom she was forever falling out. Her daughter, Hedy, just turned twenty, had been brought up mostly by our grandmother and was often deeply and unhappily in love.

Everyone was there by 9 a.m. There would be raised voices and much flapping of hands; peace and quiet were not these women's forte. Almost as soon as they arrived, they were complaining and exclaiming (a bleak and disappointed

"Oh no!" at the prospect of having to sign a check), gesticulating, shaking their heads in disappointment, twitching their feet on the carpet.

The atmosphere built up as the women's performance got under way. It was always basically the same, with minor variations introduced by some bitter new spat. They were quite detached from whatever was going on in the outside world, a tribe of women living in exile from their own country, as if on a desert island. Occasionally, and somewhat absurdly given that the din never died down, my mother would wave her fist and cry, "Be quiet now!"

Because there is no such thing as a show without an audience, I, *la petite*, bore silent witness to it all. My older brother and sister were at school. I lingered barefoot most of the morning, excused from school by a note from my mother, which she wrote by the light of an old brass lamp, sitting on a chair at her sloping bureau, clad in a pale blue robe, half-moon spectacles perched on the end of her nose. She took great care writing these notes, dipping her pen from time to time into a pot of midnight-blue ink, then rereading and fastidiously correcting the upstrokes and downstrokes of her extravagant handwriting with a loop or a horizontal line, as if pinning each letter to the page: "My daughter is rather tired today. She had a slight fever this morning. I am worried she might be coming down with something, so I have decided, as a precaution, to keep her at home today."

With my short hair and pale complexion—"You're looking green," observed my mother with a little moue of satisfaction—I was supposed, like the maids, to remain invisible. That was and had always been my designated status.

The women put on their show without ever explaining to me what was going on. It was like watching a play in a foreign language without subtitles, and I still didn't know whether it would end well or badly.

Was it all simply a cultural phenomenon? This side of the family were *pieds noirs*, whose predecessors had been among the first colonialists to settle in Algeria in the mid-nineteenth century, the poorest of the poor who had put all their hopes and aspirations into this El Dorado—at the time made up of three French departments, Algiers, Oran, and Constantine—on the other side of the Mediterranean. A century later, between the wars, they had had the bright idea of returning to mainland France, thus avoiding the catastrophe of a hasty departure thirty years later when Algeria declared its independence. Those who had waited lost everything.

This branch of the family had maintained many of the traditions of the Maghreb, one of which was the accommodation of young children in women's activities, whether at home or at the public hammam. Children would wander in and out of groups of women who were often more or less half naked and so bound up in their affairs that they paid them barely any attention.

I observed my mother, impassive, surrounded by her closest relatives, nodding her approval or chiming in with an observation as she secured a lock of hair that had escaped from the hastily pinned-up blond chignon she wore high on her head. She was not born blond, but she went blond as a young woman. Her hair was one of her few vanities. She spent long periods at the hair salon, sequestered under the helmet dryer, falling into a kind of trance, then waking with a start every so often to focus on the scandal magazine in her lap. Her hair was her identity. When she neglected it, it was a sign she was not having a good day.

She profited from the occasional lull in the daily family gatherings to write out a check for her sister, Zizi, one year and one month younger than she, to sign. Zizi was not the name on my aunt's identity card, which, moreover, she had clumsily altered to make herself younger by six years, adding a cross to the one in 1921 to make it look like she had been born, somewhat improbably, in 1927. Once again, it was up to my mother to try to sort out her sister's faux pas with the authorities. There was so much to sort out, including many parking fines affixed to my scatterbrained aunt's convertible Caravelle, which she challenged with extravagant bad faith ("This is *totally* ab-*surd*!") and which, for some mysterious reason, my father received and always ended up paying.

Zizi was petite, permanently tanned, drenched in heady perfume, with dark cropped hair that she carefully dyed and cut herself in the style of Audrey Hepburn, and possessed of a volatile temper. She dressed entirely in black: a polo-neck, regardless of the season, tight pants, high-heeled boots, and tinkling heavy silver chains and bangles. They all thought she was fanatical about housework and cleanliness, and she didn't deny it. She watched her weight, obsessed over the slightest sign of aging behind the smoky lenses of the Sophia Loren sunglasses that masked half her face, and boasted that all she kept in her refrigerator were beauty products—pots of face cream, serums, substances with English names that promised eternal youth—while my mother nagged her about third-party provisional payments and parking fines.

I understood the words *party*, *provisions*, and *parking*, but wondered what it was that might connect them. I pictured an enforcement officer dancing alongside her car as he slid the parking fine under the windshield wiper. Sometimes my mother parked her Citroën 2CV on the crosswalk outside the post office where she was popping in to withdraw some cash. She would leave me in the car with strict instructions to explain to the cop that she would be back in two minutes. The wait seemed endless. I thought I saw a police officer approaching and watched carefully for him to begin his dance. My mother arrived, out of breath—"What a dreadful queue, the wait was endless!"—and I still hadn't seen anything. She pulled the starter of the noisy 2CV and drove off, the car spluttering.

My aunt's commedia dell'arte character was tricky, while my mother's was practical. Cousin Hedy played the innocent. Hedy had something of both a naïve young girl and an unhappy woman about her. The performers, with studied gestures, elaborated their plays from a sequence of tableaux that could have been titled, like photo novels, "Disappointed Love," "Regrets for a Bygone Era," or "The Fitting Room," for in the end it always came back to clothes. The women dressed up. Each had clearly had her moment of glory, even triumph. They never bragged about it beyond their little circle, and I didn't know any details, but I could tell.

During the morning ritual, the mistress of ceremonies was always my mother, Lucie, like a ringmaster out of a Molière play. She was both the brains and the armed wing of the group, keeping the other women in check. They couldn't manage without her, but in return they insisted she knew her place. She found the endlessly repeated performances hammy and overblown. "Always the same faces, the same stories. I'd be better off reading a book," she said. Sometimes I heard her sigh.

"I know her, your mother. She can't fool me," my aunt whispered to me dramatically, refusing to say more, as she knelt to untangle the fringe that ran along the edge of the carpet, licking her index finger and then smoothing the fringe down with the flat of her hand.

The women spoke their own language. They needed to utter only a single word or part of a sentence for the meaning to be manifestly clear to the others, yet I always had the feeling they were hiding something from me. There were explanations of things I couldn't grasp or understand. It was obvious they were bound by collective memories, which they conjured up, obliquely, every single day. They had a direct line to their past.

I was fascinated by the way the other women seemed to hold sway over my mother, who behaved differently when she was with them—no longer a wife and mother, but one of them. There was a side of her that eluded me.

Lucie had, to use the professional jargon, a portfolio career with multiple roles. She liked to say that with her law degree she could have been a lawyer or a judge, but that she had always preferred to do whatsoever she pleased, whensoever she pleased. She was much sought after for her expertise, but never paid for it. As head of the apartment block's joint ownership board, she relished dropping the "homeowners' association" into conversation, with particular emphasis on the first word. To hear her, there was no homeowner quite as much of a homeowner as the head of the joint ownership board, and no meeting quite as important as the board's annual general meeting. The board (which for a long time I thought was spelled *bored*), of which she was the grande dame and principal spokesperson, came up time and again in conversation. She was always dealing with some real estate proceedings and answering a stream of telephone calls. "I saw the attorney," she would declare with a self-confident air, letting it be understood not only that she had known him for many years, but that the law was on her side.

Secular in both spirit and lifestyle, she detested churchiness, and refused to get involved in any charitable activities. She was, however, more than happy to serve as scribe for some former maid fallen on hard times, writing letters on her behalf, filling in forms required by the welfare system, listening and trying to untangle her problems. She took pleasure in the knowledge that she was the woman's superior. "Is your mother home?" I would hear as I opened the front door to yet another supplicant.

Along with her law degree she had taken a minor in biology, gaining a double degree, which she somehow made sound as if she had conducted a double life during the war. So many studies. And then nothing. Supposedly, she led an entirely bourgeois life, yet she seemed to have nothing to say to other women of her class and was quite unable to conceal her impatience when she was with them, cutting short their gossip, bringing conversations to an abrupt close, sometimes simply getting up and walking off. "Luc-ie!" her interlocutor would call after her, bewildered. It was another one of those maternal mysteries. All that education had not made her any more civilized.

Her principal occupation was doing the accounts for her sister's store, which was known rather pompously outside their circle as the "antiques emporium." In the early 1960s my aunt Zizi, who had just turned forty and was driving her friends and relatives crazy with her unfocused energy, was convinced by my mother to open an antiques store. Zizi had never studied art history, and the television was her only entertainment, but she did have, she conceded, "some nice stuff to get rid of." She kept it in the basement. "You can't pick that kind of thing up anymore. No one wants to clear out their apartment nowadays."

She liked furniture that emanated power. Everything was a "period piece," whether Directoire, Empire, or "late nineteenth century." Sometimes she would concede that a piece was a "very decent copy." The emporium was really no more than an upscale secondhand store, selling furniture from real estate foreclosures, statues from countries that turned a blind eye to illegal exports, curios my aunt picked up at flea markets, and jewelry my mother purchased by weight at municipal credit auctions, saying confusingly that she had obtained the jewelry from "my aunt." Zizi mostly sold her stock to other women. There was no postpurchase service. No one was going to get their hands on her nice little earnings. Any unhappy customer was swiftly shown the door.

My mother also did her sister's tax return and negotiated adjustments with the taxman. "I have that dear little inspector eating out of my hand," she said cheerfully, apparently convinced that right up until the mid-1960s every functionary could be bribed, and a deal could be struck on every tax bill. My mother begged him to understand: she was helping out her sister, who was a little feebleminded. "You and your sister," the inspector repeated, as if they were one and the same person.

As she dealt with time-consuming bureaucratic chores, the ladies sat around flapping their hands in her living room, most of the time clad in little more than panties, panty hose, and brassieres. Their panty hose, squeezed tight at the waist, were often darned and not very becoming. Their brassieres had seen better days. There was nothing erotic about the intimate displays of these women—one in her seventies, two in their forties, and my twenty-year-old cousin—but I found it all endlessly intriguing.

At 9 a.m. on the dot, the women turned up for their peculiar rituals. They were fully made-up, laden with jewelry, ready to perform. Yet the moment they entered the apartment they began to remove their clothes, as if preparing to put on a different costume. The time they spent in their undergarments was worthy of a doctor's examination room—"Please get undressed and someone will be along to get you." It was so protracted it was almost as if the trying on of clothes that followed was merely a pretext. They had come over to parade, self-satisfied and half naked. In performance, in competition, they were like actresses, except that I was their only audience. My mother offered them no refreshments. The sessions always took place in the morning. For a long time, I believed that the expression "at the theater" referred to the early part of the day.

The maid was in the apartment but confined to the kitchen, and plainly despised by the ladies' club—the only thing they could bring themselves to say about her was that she "smelled very strongly under the arms." My mother underpaid a succession of very young women who came from the countryside, mostly from Nièvre, Calvados, or Mayenne, whom she usually picked out from the produce stall at the market.

"You haven't got one of your girls for me, do you? She'll get board and lodging and I'll sort her out shorthand lessons. She'll have her afternoons to herself." Often as good as illiterate, these girls put up with my mother's fits of rage and stayed until they got married, unless they "did wrong," in which case they were immediately sent packing, picked up and taken home by a brutal father. They were servants in the real sense of the term, who lived with us and were granted Sundays off. The advantage of an illiterate maid, my mother seemed to think, was that she understood nothing and did not speak unless spoken to.

At around 11 a.m. Lucie announced it was time to call it a day and she was off to get properly dressed. The other women prepared to leave, making an unsolicited detour through the kitchen. They stood at the open refrigerator and filled their faces like hamsters. Unlike my mother, they did not know how to cook: my grandmother survived on café au lait and tapioca as she had in Algeria, my aunt on tea and biscuits, and my cousin ate anything.

After the women left, in the empty hours of the day, my mother would make me recite my irregular German verbs. *Backen, buk, gebacken*: "to bake." "Again. Good. You know it now." Bremen, Hamburg, Stettin; the Weser, the Elbe, and the Oder. I chorused after her the names of cities and rivers I could not locate on a map. I learned about Mendel's laws. Dominant and recessive genes. The strong and the weak. The example of blue eyes: if you have blue eyes, it means you don't have a recessive brown-eye gene.

All this was, apparently, my due. My legacy. My mother was endlessly boasting about my "intelligence," encouraging me but never explaining why. It was as if she were signaling to me, "You'll figure it out on your own, even if I can't tell you what it is." When I think of those years, I picture myself always at the same age, wearing my white cotton nightgown with its little broderie anglaise ruff. I liked to sit, protected by it, sniffing my knees. Watching.

Some years later, my mother got into the habit of preparing an "evening soup" for everyone, a ritual that would come to be considered perfectly normal, even expected. My aunt would drop by on her way home from the antiques store and slurp it down greedily, perched on a stool in the kitchen, before leaving without saying goodbye; my cousin would arrive and serve herself without asking. The time for interminable chatter was long past.

After a few years, I was put in charge of taking the soup over to my grandmother, who still lived in the right-hand wing of the circle formed by the three buildings. Pushing open the front door to her apartment, I would find her lying on her bed half naked—this was, clearly, a habit—having just given herself a shot of morphine, the needle still lodged in her buttock. "Adorable Herminette," as my mother called her disingenuously, had crazy hair that made her look like Baba Yaga, the witch in the Russian fairy tale.

She would tell me, not very nicely, to go away and leave her alone. She had become dependent on opiates after being prescribed them in the wake of a painful operation. Her craving for them steadily increased, and now she could no longer do without. There were enough doctors in her entourage to indulge her with prescriptions. She wandered around her overheated apartment in a petticoat, doing nothing more than trying to avoid what she called "a collapse," an agonizing attack that now occurred more and more frequently, sending her limbs into spasm. She called it her Saint Vitus's dance. I would take the soup, untouched, back up to our apartment. My mother didn't want to hear about it. It was enough that she fed all these people, just as she had "during the Occupation."

Sometimes she told me about the train to Burgundy she took at dawn, the local man waiting for her at the station, the back of his van filled with lumps of coal. The journey back to Paris that same evening, carrying all the "butter-eggs-cheese" she had been able to persuade her cousins to give her. Twice a month, Lucie kept the family warmed and fed.

Any woman who was introduced to the family had to submit to the gynaeceum's morning rituals. This happened to my brother's first wife in 1970. She was encouraged to take off her clothes on the pretext that she had come over to try on some clothes. The young woman, not yet twenty, shy and confused, was scrutinized like a young filly by expert eyes. In her role of the new Naïve in the gynaeceum's commedia dell'arte, she was felt up by hands as expert as those of a brothel madam. The way she responded dictated what was said about her. She was deemed "excellent." Or not.

The women were not very pleasant even to one another.

"Sit up straight, you look like a hunchback."

"Pull your stomach in."

"I'm so swollen, I'm bulging out of my corset."

They swapped clothes, then grabbed them back. No gift was definitive. "Look at this Liberty-print blouse. Why don't you try it on? It fits you like a glove. Be careful taking it off!"—as if the most important thing about an item of clothing was its removal. It looked good when worn, but just as good unworn.

Then there were the words I heard uttered in one breath as if they formed a single word: "It's-a-gift-from-Martine." Martine was a friend and customer of my aunt who lived nearby.

"She didn't wear it even once, she's *always* buying clothes she never wears." According to my aunt, Martine had a private income, and she purchased everything Zizi showed her in the store. She often spent the entire afternoon there, chatting, drinking tea, and munching the dry little biscuits Zizi rather meanly offered her.

"I love a little nibble," my aunt would pretend, picking up a crumb from the floor and bringing it to her lips. Martine bought things without bargaining, barely even looking at them, and then, not content with having paid top dollar, came back with a bag of clothes for Zizi that she claimed she had no more use for. My aunt, twenty years her senior, would listen as she recounted yet another messy saga, interrupting every so often with indignant exclamations. "Men! Unbelievable. How *dare* he!"

It seemed to me that Martine's problem was not men so much as the fact that she was an only child whose parents were dead, and everyone was after her money. My aunt knew all about that, including the story of the family's hôtel particulier in the 16th arrondissement of Paris that had, puzzlingly, been turned into a prison camp during the Occupation. What Occupation? Who were the prisoners? Obviously, I never wondered this aloud. This was just one of the things left unsaid in my family; everyone was convinced that if things remained unspoken they did not exist. No one wanted to talk about the past except in vague generalizations that piqued my curiosity. Was it because Martine's parents were dead that my aunt displayed such solicitude toward her, even while fleecing her unscrupulously of her money? Or was Zizi deliberately abusing her psychologically to get at her money, as though it were her due? My aunt was devious but not too bright, sentimental but not very sensitive; she always made out she was acting simply by instinct and intuition, two terms she employed without distinction. She was influenced by the signs of the zodiac. "I am a Scorpio," she would declare assertively. "I'm particularly suited to Virgos." She never specified if they were men or women.

In truth, nothing about Martine and their other benefactors was neutral in the eyes of the clan. Among themselves, they exaggerated the pronunciation of these women's surnames as a way of reminding the assembled company—in case there was the slightest doubt—that they were Jewish, and thus, by definition, wealthy. And because these meetings were private, just family, recalling this was also a way of remembering, keeping the flame alive, reinforcing their loyalty to the clan. Meanwhile, nothing was made of the fact that these Jewish procurers—even now that they were adults—were orphans. Their parents had died, but how? When I asked, I was told they had been "deported," a term whose meaning was vague to me, halfway between *departed* and *transported*. Where to? And why did they die? My mother gave me a long-winded answer that I didn't really understand. She made the cold, bureaucratic information sound self-evident. Apparently this was the way things were for Jews. And Jews were, well, Jews.

Obviously no one ever mentioned genocide or the Holocaust, words I learned later from books. The women talked about "the war" as if the generic term was sufficient to account for the fate of individuals.

Martine's function was, naturally, to be extravagant. That was the role of Jews in general: to give away, to part with their possessions. "Martine is so generous!" It was said with a hint of contempt. Truly, she was useless at managing and holding on to her money.

She committed suicide at the age of twenty-six, after a brief, unhappy marriage, celebrated in the Saint-Eustache church in Paris one freezing cold Saturday afternoon in December in the early 1970s. My mother and I were invited to the gloomy ceremony. Martine stood rapt before the altar, for once very slim, in a long white dress with a train and a sort of white bonnet with feathers that looked like something out of *Swan Lake*. The groom, older than she was, seemed distracted. The Franciscan priest kept waving his hands around in irritation. There were not many other guests. They divorced soon after.

My aunt sounded upset, even slightly annoyed, when she talked about her young benefactor's death. She seemed mostly disappointed about the loss of the horn of plenty that had provided her with a steady stream of new clothes at no cost. With each new delivery she would toss the garments theatrically onto the floor, spreading them over the carpet in the middle of the ladies' circle. The tribe would fall upon them, squabbling, pulling them on and tearing them off one another without a shred of modesty, sometimes layering several garments on top of one another. It was like an organized pillage, unbounded greed. *Martine was always so generous!*

The women closed ranks against the outside world. I had my place among them, as long as I didn't get in the way. Every so often my mother would call on me for support: "You see! *La petite* agrees!" she would declare triumphantly.

They grumbled, declared this or that person a "dirty bastard," disappeared into the kitchen to binge, returning with their mouths full to try on a garment or set off a scene, leaving a trail of life in their wake. So-and-so was performing at the theater, they had tickets, they mentioned the names of people I had never met. Someone had given them two opera tickets and left their name at the box office. They all seemed to live off a ticket gleaned here and there. They posed like goddesses in their shabby underwear. They were phobic about everything ("I cannot abide sickness," warned my aunt), and treated every little twinge with comical remedies: charcoal, broth, hot water bottles, glycerin suppositories, aspirin, talcum powder, Vichy water, or lozenges. Cancer and depression were for other people.

They spent an awful lot of time discussing men, though men barely seemed to figure in their lives. Only my mother was married and apparently contented, and the tribe did all it could to remind her, not without a certain smugness as well as a touch of jealousy, of her other great love affair, with a man who had died tragically toward the end of the war. They alluded to him in veiled terms. Once I stumbled upon an identity card dated 1943 in one of the drawers in my mother's desk, whose black-and-white photograph showed a smiling, clearly recognizable young woman: my mother. But the surname was different. It was a huge shock, especially as, rather than enlighten me, Lucie simply began to cry. I deduced from this that it was safer not to ask any questions. According to the tribe, her second husband had only ever played second fiddle to this other man. He had fathered her children, that was all. They feared and disliked him but were unable to make him go away.

My aunt Zizi was not interested in men, though she loved being taken out and pampered, preferably by "pederasts," as she called them. When one invited her to join him for an evening at the opera to "bring an end to the rumors"—this was before the 1981 law decriminalizing homosexuality—she began getting dolled up first thing in the morning, excited to be seen at his side and to help him pull the wool over people's eyes. She did it with women too. Just once, my aunt took me aside and confided, "It's so nice falling asleep with my friend, cuddled up against her." This particular friend, an androgenous blond who shared her first name, was a "regular," until the inevitable rancorous falling out, just as with all the others. The gynaeceum, by tacit agreement, refrained from commenting on the vagaries of my aunt's friendships. My mother sighed. She would be stuck with her sister forever.

My grandmother was well past the age for such activities, but she was of the era when men and women had specific roles to play. Cousin Hedy, meanwhile, was constantly veering from one broken heart to yet another terrible choice of boyfriend, all of which was extensively discussed by the gynaeceum. She didn't seem likely to be married off anytime soon.

The other women were quite happy with the absence of men in their lives and tried to draw my mother further into their cenacle. The things they said about men sounded bitter. I once overheard them quoting Flaubert, "The finest roosters never run to fat." Did virility mean that a man had to go on a diet to avoid ending up as a capon? They'd had ten years to "settle down," as they put it—to find a fat wallet and a stallion embodied in one and the same person.

The gynaeceum may have addressed one another as sweetheart, darling, *ma petite*, but they were really very catty to one another. Occasionally, one of the weaker links—usually my cousin—would march off, slamming the door behind her, and stay away for hours or days. *La Naïve* was not the sharpest tool in the box. Her limited horizons did not stretch beyond getting her *baccalauréat*, which my mother patiently sat her down to review for, then a bit of studying some foreign language, as was the fashion at the time, and that was it. She was older than I was—born just after the Liberation—and wore her name, Hedy, spotted on an American tank, almost like an alibi. The idea of naming her Hedwig had been briefly considered. She looked like a sort of grown-up Shirley Temple, with ringlets tied with pink bows and a slightly robotic smile. Although I didn't think she was fat, there was constant talk of her going on a new diet, each more improbable than the last. These women positively tortured one another. After a few weeks of torment, my cousin would step onto the scale and burst into tears as she saw she had yet again failed to lose any weight—the opposite, in fact. How could Hedy believe her mother? Trust her aunt? Rely on her grandmother's advice? The might of the group was stronger than she was.

Conversations often took a personal turn. "Your daughter's carrying too much puppy fat," my aunt would say to my mother, referring to my unfortunate elder sister. "I shall take her to see the masseur Noneste. And Alfonso." Alfonso called himself a dancer but was really a gymnastics teacher. "He does me a world of good, he hangs me up by my hands and pulls. I can hear my bones crack. And she needs to get her teeth fixed. Maurice has given me such a pretty smile. Look." Maurice was her dentist, blind in one eye.

Endlessly discontented, the women scrutinized one another like courtesans, seeking out the slightest imperfection. All they had was their bodies, and it was their bodies that spoke for them. I dreamed of seeing them like Phryne, the Greek courtesan who bares herself before her judges and wins them over with her naked beauty.

Despite all this, somehow they were in harmony. Their relationship was the fabric of their existence, their bond the essence of their lives. A favorite story was about a woman they knew who had such a long line of descendants she could say, "My daughter, go and tell your daughter that her daughter's daughter is crying." They loved this idea of generations bequeathing their tears, without knowing why.

In conversation, my aunt took the shouting part, my mother the bass harmony, and my cousin seemed to be trying to imitate them both. The three of them spoke over one another in chorus:

"Will you look at these bulges!" (My aunt tilting her pelvis to expose her belly and pinching a roll of fat.)

"See this cellulite? I've been massaging it with a horsehair glove." (My cousin ostentatiously frowning at a lumpy thigh.)

"She had a nose job at Judat's clinic. He's an excellent surgeon." (I misheard and thought my aunt had said *Judas*.)

"I'm getting crow's-feet too." (My mother peering into the magnifying mirror a few centimeters away from her face.)

"Do you think I need a face-lift? I'm starting to look like a turkey." (My aunt pinching her neck—imperative not to answer.)

The conversation would move on from aesthetic concerns to conjugal issues, essentially revolving around infidelity, a lover (also referred to as a "chap" or a "fellow"), or a mistress.

"He's dumped his wife. That bitch got her hooks into him. She made him agree to a divorce." "She's a kept woman" was the ultimate insult.

The conversation would turn to oblique talk of gynecological problems. Any mention of abortion was taboo in my presence. My mother would occasionally order the tribe, in English (which I didn't understand), to "*Stop talking!*" in an exaggerated accent that overestimated by far her audience's linguistic abilities. The other women would look at her, frowning, uncertain if they had understood anything except possibly the word *stop*, the one word I too had understood. They would lower their eyes and obey. Once again, they had gone too far.

In coded language, the conversation went, "I have a friend who had a little problem. I gave her the number of this marvelous doctor I know."

Or, "That nice pharmacist gave *la petite*"—that was me—"the package for Maman." My grandmother nodded.

What was in the package? Potions to bring about abortions, black soap, rubber cords, addictive substances. I was a messenger of death. I never dared open the carefully sealed paper bag handed to me by the pharmacy technician.

They sometimes brought up my maternal grandparents' former home, a small two-room apartment on the first floor of a block in the 15th arrondissement, which they had rented between the wars, after their return from Algeria. It was near the Bir-Hakeim bridge, opposite a structure called the Vélodrome d'Hiver.

The women mentioned the "Vél d'Hiv roundup" in a matter-of-fact way, mostly in terms of the heat wave that had hit Paris in mid-July 1942. "The Jews were taken there by bus," they said. It was stiflingly hot. There was an enormous mass of people inside the velodrome and the tumult could be heard through the glass roof. Through a gap in the enclosure, a Jewish man had handed my grandmother a gold watch in exchange for a glass of water. My grandmother took the watch but did not bring him the water. It was said with no emotion. I wondered if I had heard right.

Conversation inevitably turned to Uncle Gaston, whose first and last names were always uttered in one breath. His surname was the same as ours, but the family relationship was never clarified. He was an "important journalist," editorial director of *Paris-Soir*, a "serious newspaper." These were, as far as they were concerned, hard facts.

On the evening of the Vél d'Hiv roundup, on July 16th, Uncle Gaston, in quest of a scoop, paid a visit to his cousins. There had been a brief thunderstorm, but it was still unbearably muggy. It was chaos inside the Vél d'Hiv, which by now the whole of Paris knew about—there was nothing new to tell the newspaper's readers. But the important journalist had a job to do. If Parisians wanted information, they would have it. Gaston took a bird's-eye view photograph—not credited to him, of course—of the exterior of the Vél d'Hiv. He climbed to the top of the apartment building, all the way up to the servants' quarters. From there, leaning out of the window, he could see the entrance to the Vél d'Hiv and the empty buses parked all down the street. Like the good son of a cop he was, his initial thought was, "Move along now, nothing to see here." It is the only known photograph of the Vél d'Hiv roundup. This was said with pride. The story ended there.

Little more was said in the family circle about this compromising relative who bore the same surname as they, apart from the fact that he had died relatively young in Switzerland.

Years later, when I became a historian, I began researching the man I thought was my great-uncle. I discovered he had been an acquaintance of Otto Abetz, the Reich's (the tribe pronounced it *Rèche*) ambassador to Paris. He was on first-name terms with Jean Luchaire, head of the powerful Corporation Nationale de la Presse. Although as a young man he had been a socialist, during the Occupation he played a central role in influencing French public opinion in favor of the Nazis, as a strategic and shrewd journalist promoting the ideology of his new German masters. He carefully dosed his antisemitism according to the organ he was writing for. His range was broad: not only was he editor of the supposedly serious *Paris-Soir*, he also contributed to the rabidly antisemitic weekly newspapers *Gringoire* and *Je suis partout*, and the French edition of the Nazi propaganda magazine *Signal*.

Better yet, Gaston became a newly minted media baron. In mid-June 1940, in an occupied and largely deserted Paris, he seized his chance. The German authorities appointed him editorial director of *Paris-Soir*, replacing Pierre Lazareff, who had been forced into exile in the United States.

Before the war, as an employee in the billboard division at the SFIO, the French Section of the Workers' International, Gaston had gotten a sense of how propaganda campaigns worked. He knew to remain the soul of discretion, ensuring any reference to him in the collaborationist press mentioned only his position, never his name. He published freelance articles under either his initials or a pseudonym; eventually half the inhabitants of the village where he was born had authored his articles, the fact of which they were entirely unaware. It kept him entertained.

Lazareff had been blocking his path for a long time. In all honesty, the fall of France had come at the perfect time for Gaston, who had been fantasizing about rising to editor-in-chief for a while. There was some muttering that the editors of newspapers published after 1940 were corrupt, carefully selected by the Germans who needed them to be compliant while under their command. Some even dared to claim there was nothing easier than being promoted to editor. It was true, of course, that the Germans kept a close eye on things. But twenty-five thousand francs a month! They were just envious. He'd have liked to see them doing his job.

Gaston was in favor of the New Order. Jews had inveigled themselves into every walk of life; it was time to be done with them, all those politicians and newspapermen and movie types claiming they were being persecuted. Some of his colleagues had joined the Association of Anti-Jewish Journalists. The AJA was legal. Entirely aboveboard.

Even once he became editor, Gaston had to bide his time

for nine long years. When his time eventually came, the daily newspaper, under his direction, became an accommodating blend of news and propaganda. There were new sections of interest to everyone: appeals for news of people and possessions missing or mislaid during the exodus of June 1940; the "Messages" section, for families; maps showing the location of prisoners of war in Germany. It all created the impression of providing a service to readers, although the real purpose was to get them accustomed to their German masters. A shrewd propagandist for the new regime, he worked hard to ensure that the newspaper's circulation—two million copies a day—barely dipped. *Paris-Soir* was still the people's newspaper: Gaston never forgot his roots. After all, didn't the term National Socialist include the word *socialist*? The fervent French republican had simply slipped a little to the right. Hadn't Pierre Laval himself also started out in the SFIO?

Thanks to his connections, the serious newspaper began to circulate again almost immediately after the armistice. True, the agency that supplied its news was now German, but there were plenty of ways of getting along with the censors. If other newspapers were sold with words and sentences blacked out, sometimes even entirely empty columns right in the middle of the page, they had only themselves to blame. Gaston knew how to outmaneuver the entire system: censorship, paper supply, and distribution.

The new editorial director had introductions everywhere, from the *Propagandastaffel*, the German propaganda service, to the Reich's embassy. His relatives also benefited from his new status; they shared the same surname, which was now a source of pride. Everyone profited, according to their requirements and their inclinations. My grandfather, who had been imprisoned in a stalag, was released at the end of 1941. My mother, Lucie, serious, hardworking, and not particularly worldly, was employed in the propaganda service, where she progressed rapidly under the aegis of her uncle. My grandmother and my aunt Zizi were received everywhere: they were surprised and delighted to find themselves socializing with *le Tout Paris*, the Parisian smart set. The collaborationist smart set, of course. Not that there was any other kind.

I have found photographs of them in the Nazi propaganda magazine *Signal*, beginning in the summer of 1940 right up until spring 1944, posing in full-page and sometimes double-page spreads at receptions at the Reich's embassy, or taking carriage rides in the Bois de Boulogne. They were frivolity incarnate. The only restriction Gaston imposed was that their names were not to be published. Intoxicated by their new and unexpected glory, they nonetheless had no choice but to comply. Nicknamed "two beautiful women of mystery," they returned home every night to their little two-room apartment like a pair of Cinderellas.

Midway through the Occupation, as he sensed the tide beginning to turn, Uncle Gaston gradually began to adopt a lower profile. By the time of the Liberation, he only ever talked about his frankly minimal Resistance activities, thanks to which he was left in peace, but at the age of forty-nine his career in journalism was over. His important newspaper was now proscribed as a collaborationist mouthpiece. Lazareff, its former editorial director, returned from exile, founded another newspaper, and appointed an editor-in-chief. Gaston became a press historian—an object lesson in how to rewrite history without mentioning his own—and a professor at a school of journalism. One cannot both be and have been.

The women of the gynaeceum never got over their former glory. As though the shift in France's fortunes was due solely to the return of Lazareff, the now invincible press baron, all my aunt would say about him was a decisive "How I detest that little man!"

And so the group always returned to the heart of the matter: "The bastards!" The women began to chirrup, the conversation grew heated, voices were raised.

"And now them . . . with their po-*lice* . . . their *jus*-tice . . . Why do they want to drag us through the shit—?" my aunt exploded with sudden fury, swiftly tempered by a glance from my mother. Lucie went further, but her tone was calmer: "Quite. Were we supposed to let them be the only ones permitted to enjoy themselves?" She spoke with a firm conviction that was reflected in her expression, but I simply could not figure out who "they" were. The rich? The Germans? My cousin Hedy, with nothing to say on the subject, kept making irrelevant points in her shrill little voice.

The women liked to scare themselves. They spoke with contagious fear about "terrorists" (were they the same as "bastards"?) lurking in the *quartiers rouges*, the communist neighborhoods in the north and east of Paris. For my mother, the Marais and the Faubourg Saint-Antoine formed a sort of frontier beyond which she rarely ventured unless she was going to buy fabric at the Marché Saint-Pierre in Montmartre. I spotted the word *Dreyfus* printed on bright blue paper packaging.

When they were in a calmer mood, my mother and aunt reminisced about the good times, fitting recompense for the days they'd worked their fingers to the bone to pay the bills. Living by their wits, they called it. To listen to them, the Occupation had been a fairy-tale period. Enigmatically, they said, "We didn't miss out on anything." It took me many years to understand what they meant.

"Do you remember that lovely white organdie dress I wore to that party at the embassy?" (I figured out eventually they meant the German embassy, but they were tight-lipped about the details. They had been invited to the Hôtel de Beauharnais, Rue de Lille, in Saint-Germain-des-Prés. That was all I could squeeze out of them.)

"That little hôtel particulier in the 16th arrondissement." (As if they were playing *Monopoly*—a *hôtel particulier* being something between a grand house and an aristocratic mansion—like a building being given back after it was taken from them.)

"You remember that pretty cherrywood half-moon table I helped myself to?" (Said in a little girl's tone of false contrition. I threw a discreet glance at the apartment's mute furniture.)

"There were so many bargains to be had. You made an

offer, you could take whatever you wanted. Everyone was buying and selling; it was literally as simple as that. There's always been robberies. The Jews are exaggerating, as ever." (The tone was brisk.)

As much as they could, they avoided uttering the word Jew. On the rare occasions they did, it was with a mixture of disgust and intense fascination: "He's a Jew." That seemed to be all they had to say, but I wondered if it was an insult. My mother talked about "the chosen people" (chosen by whom, I wondered) or "assimilated Jews," conjuring up the image of a secret conspiracy, with no distinctive outward sign. She talked about Freemasons too, of course. Around the time of the revolution of May 1968, my mother began to cite, with a knowing look, de Gaulle's famous description of the Jews as an "elite people, self-confident, and domineering." She seemed to feel legitimated.

There was a lot of circumlocution. "A sign of his Jewishness" meant quite simply, "He's got a long nose." "She has the look," or, more rarely, "the Semitic look," translated as "She's Jewish."

Unluckily for the all the Cinderellas, midnight was about to chime. In 1944 "the bastards" entered Paris like a swarm of locusts and brought the Occupation—the good times, in other words—to an end. The young women's carriage turned into a pumpkin. "The bastards ruined it all," my aunt lamented in her nasal whine. It was the end of everything. Rather than talking about the Allies (whose allies were they, I wondered), she spoke of the Americans as if she were describing a tourism strategy to encourage the to-ing and fro-ing of people who preferred the mountains to the beach. I could never work out who were the good guys and who were the bad.

Everything always ended with my cousin's piercing shrieks, or the muffled sound of my aunt pacing across the carpet, or someone hanging up the telephone in fury.

Whenever an outsider entered the circle (usually my father), everyone froze. "Here comes Charles," someone would whisper like an alarm signal. The women would scatter at his approach like a flock of blackbirds that had been pecking at the ground. All anger and resentment were swallowed up instantly. My mother furiously wiped away her tears, my aunt declared she was off to the antique store, and my cousin vanished, slamming the door behind her. All that remained was the heavy and electric atmosphere, and my father looking around in bafflement.

Now the day could begin.

The rituals of the gynaeceum went on for decades, continuing long after I left home. None of the women was ever absent for long, except when they went on vacation, and even then they found themselves unable to leave one another's side completely. Nonetheless, the tradition gradually faded away. At the end of the 1970s, my grandmother's body finally gave up and she died in the hospital. My mother suffered a fatal heart attack at home some years later. My aunt did not survive her for very long.

Years hence, Hedy was still in the habit of dropping by my parents' apartment, treating it as though it were an empty space, even though my father, now old and sick, was still living there. Often, when I went to visit him, I would hear from a distance the sound of a front door slamming shut. It was her. She never came to say hello. The refrigerator was empty. The concierge had been told not to give her the keys, which she swore she had returned, but for many years there were multiple duplicates in circulation.

2

IN THE WINTER OF 1940, at a party in Paris for medical students, Lucie met a man called Friedrich. She had just turned twenty-one; he was twenty-four. Friedrich was from Alsace and had been ostracized by his prominent Catholic family. He looked like a modern-day Siegfried: tall, lanky, blond hair slicked back, high cheekbones; he had clearly not been born into the *Lumpenproletariat*. With his jacket draped over his shoulders, he was a very attractive young man.

Lucie was also tall and slim. She had recently begun to go blond, and her hair was growing gradually lighter with the advance of the German Army. She was vivacious, with an impish expression and a strong nose.

Friedrich was hoping to become a researcher in genetic biology, a promising specialty for someone interested in exploring racial science. He was completing his medical studies in Paris, where he worked as a laboratory assistant at the Collège de France, a prestigious research establishment. His doctoral thesis focused on the "yellow body" or the *corpus luteum* that can form in the ovaries, and he was particularly interested in hormonal function, specifically the endocrine glands. Lucie was studying law, about which she was indifferent, but she was ambitious to succeed.

Not long after they entered each other's lives, Lucie moved in with Friedrich, near the Jardin des Plantes, on Rue Cuvier, named for the renowned anatomist. They were young, and they made a fashionable couple; they could have been models for the photographer of the day, Hoyningen-Huene. Elegant, dynamic, and inseparable, they shared the same ideas, the same ambitions, and the same values. All it took was one of them to think something for the other to say it.

Lucie was an enthusiast. She always had been. Energetic too. Since her teens, in the Burgundy village of Les Chomettes, she had enjoyed an active love life in tandem with her studies. By the time she turned fifteen, she had already been taking lessons, as it were, with a local teacher, and she continued her erotic apprenticeship through a variety of encounters, always careful to ensure, since she was still a minor, that her father remained unaware.

When she met Friedrich, Lucie was enjoying a love affair, as blithe as it was ideological, with a lieutenant in the *Kommandantur*. Her *Standortkommandant* came from East Prussia in Greater Germany and was in charge of housing. In other words, he had long-term plans. Their first formal encounter was in Les Chomettes; as the mayor's granddaughter, Lucie had been instructed to welcome the officer during an inspection of his men, who were being lodged with various local families. Lucie and her German cavalier grew close, and they took to riding beautiful Trakehner horses through the Burgundy countryside, in full view of the locals. It was through him and his pillow talk that "Luzie," his "darling L," had her first encounter with German fascism.

(I never heard Lucie talk about or display her equestrian prowess, though she had a pair of tall polished boots in fawn leather that she liked to wear, a little incongruously, about town.)

The *Leutnant* did what he could to sweeten Lucie's life, allowing her to pocket the rental income from a small apartment in the next town that had been requisitioned and conveniently reassigned to Mademoiselle Lucie. She was supposed to collect the rent every month and sign the receipt in the requisition ledger, but she was capricious, and though at first she collected the rent regularly, she grew increasingly erratic about keeping the appointment. She had so much else to do!

The love affair left her with a quirky taste for onomastics and etymology. More significantly, she developed a fascination for the *Burgund* Project, whereby her native region of Burgundy was to become an autonomous state under control of the SS security service, within the Reich, as part of the New Order of Europe.

The Burgundians have been Celts since the fourth century AD. They have been French since Lothair II, the great-grandson of Charlemagne, founded the kingdom of Lotharingia. Though the new capital was to be Saint-Florentin, not Lucie's birthplace, Les Chomettes, which was too obscure, Lucie was already picturing herself as First Lady of the First Village. *Signal* magazine published stories with photographic portraits of the village's hoary old winegrowers, whose light eyes and luxuriant moustaches seemed to support this new division of territory. Lucie's own family were known for their pale blue eyes, which indicated they possessed Germanic blood, and were therefore most suitable for rebuilding *Burgund*. The whole thing was to be accompanied by a population transfer. Displacement was the order of the day. In the name of the Greater Germanic Reich, Tyroleans would come and settle in the region and place-names would be changed.

Lucie herself had dark eyes, not the perfect Aryan type. When asked, she would explain that eye color is a question of dominant and recessive genes, meaning that even if it didn't look like it, she did have the blue gene. Her eyes were blue on the inside, that was all. It was not just a question of color; it was about the whole person. What mattered was having the gene, even if it was hidden.

The discovery of Nazi ideology had been a profound shock, the total, all-encompassing, systemic thought being developed on the other side of the Rhine, irrigating life, death, science, culture, politics, and behavior. And because the Reich was going to win the war, its promise was about to become a reality.

Lucie's handsome German officer was transferred to a barracks outside Paris. From time to time he was able to take leave and Lucie would go up to the capital to show him around the City of Light. Her German lover was serious—there were vows, declarations, pledges. But soon he was sent to the Eastern Front, never to return.

Until meeting him, Lucie had come across only French fascism, a disorganized and motley mix of antirepublican nationalism, resentment, anarchism, and xenophobia. The anti-parliamentary demonstration on Place de la Concorde on February 6th, 1934, had been a missed opportunity: they should have crossed the bridge and taken the National Assembly, a hundred yards away. They failed to seize power—but this was not to be the fascists' final word.

Lucie may have been antirepublican, but she was an emblematic product of republican meritocracy. Born into relative poverty—a fact from which she drew a kind of pride—her scholastic career was impeccable: she finished top of the class at the village school, gained the highest grade in the whole region on her school certificate, and was awarded a scholarship to attend high school in Paris. An achievement paradigmatic of France's Third Republic, which did not, however, assuage her desire to even the score; quite the opposite in fact, for she discovered in Paris that it wasn't enough to be intelligent, brilliant even, to succeed. At one of the most elite high schools in the capital, the little country girl from Burgundy was mocked by her Parisian classmates. She quickly shed her accent. But she would have her revenge. Her schoolmates, from well-to-do families, were almost all Jewish. She had found her target. Lucie would have the last laugh.

Her new lover, Friedrich, was there to help her rise socially; together, with their intelligence, they would become masters of the new world.

Thanks to shifting borders, Friedrich had changed nationality several times since he was born. Born German during World War I, he became French two years later, after the armistice; aged twenty-three, he became German again, after the annexation of Alsace in July 1940. He spoke both languages, was at ease in both cultures, and it was with full knowledge of the facts that he chose to follow the path to the New Order.

His parents chose France. For him, to align oneself with France was to align oneself with the losing side, crushed by the Wehrmacht and forced to sign the Armistice agreement. France had chosen the Europe of yesterday rather than the Europe of tomorrow. He had, quite naturally, chosen Hitler's Germany, which was taking its revenge and had the dynamism to confront any challenge. The Reich proposed a coherent vision of society: everything was to be restructured and built anew. In reaction to his parents, and embracing the spirit of the times, Friedrich became an eager convert to the Nazi cause. Germany was a wonderland of modern medicine and science. Zoology, laboratories, and the microscope were all German innovations. Chemistry too—all those Nobel Prizes! So many exciting prospects.

Biology was the path to the most prestigious careers. German society was no longer conceptualizing in terms of simple biology but in terms of race, blood, and genetics, using the fundamental laws of nature to organize law, war, sex, international relations, and the supreme science of medicine. New avenues of biological research were consolidating the supremacy of medicine over all other sciences. Biology was the science of race, not simply of living organisms: living organisms structured according to racial laws. The racial laws had a reassuring aspect; you just had to be on the right side, and he was. Jews were to be treated like tubercular bacilli. Is there anything in nature as aggressive, blind, and hostile as a virus, a bacillus, a bacterium?

Friedrich's official first name was Josef. Like Goebbels. All the men in his family were given Josef as a first name—to distinguish between them they were called by a diminutive: Sepp, Seppi, Seppala. The problem was that Josef was a Jewish name. Friedrich decided to use his second name, the Christian name of German emperors and kings. Friedrich Barbarossa, Emperor Redbeard; Friedrich von Hohenstaufen, Frederick II, Holy Roman Emperor; Friedrich der Grosse, King of Prussia; Friedrich the Great. The list went on. Josef on the other hand—who was called Josef? There was Emperor Joseph II, of course, but Josef with an *f*? Apart from his glorious contemporary and almost colleague, the Bavarian-born Mengele, whose work he was yet to come across.

He hesitated over what to call himself, but once he got to Paris he began going by Friedrich. That was what Lucie called him. Sometimes Ferry. But never Josef. After the Occupation began in June 1940, he was amply rewarded for his decision and confirmed in his vocation: Almost immediately a laboratory assistant position became available at the Collège de France, occasioned by the forced departure of a young Jewish man, François Jacob. Friedrich seized the opportunity and took over Jacob's experiments on mice. He was hoping to become a geneticist. He already felt like the master of the world, although for the moment, working at his bench, he was only the master of his mice, and a few laboratory rabbits.

He joined a team led by Professor Robert Courrier, whose research focused on reproductive biology. A specialist in sexual endocrinology, Courrier was trying to isolate female hormones. Researching an impossible-to-locate follicle, Friedrich repeated his animal experiments over and over as he worked on his thesis. Courrier had come to Paris from the Strasbourg School, the newly Germanized Babylon, where he, like Friedrich, had studied at the school of medicine. Friedrich was certainly on the best path to becoming a biologist working on the classification of living tissue. Since the first German annexation after the Franco-Prussian War of 1870, the faculties in both Nancy and Strasbourg had benefited from a significant influx of money and were now home to a large number of research departments. Courrier's department had multiplied its requirements as well as its faddish interests.

Friedrich had no interest in treating the sick. He preferred human tissue to human beings. A good National Socialist, he fully adhered to its ideology and made sure to disseminate it to those around him: allegiance to Germanic faith, tradition, heroism, and the study of nature. He was always using unfamiliar words whose meanings Lucie would furtively look up in her etymological dictionary. *Holistic*, for example, came from the Greek *holos*, meaning "whole." She understood that the *Volk* was primordial: it was only the *people* who could establish laws and norms, which were dictated by the *soul of the people*. Her family was socialist, or it used to be. That was why proverbs and traditions were so important. They could be used to codify rights in accordance with race.

Lucie was rather taken by the notion of popular wisdom, even if, secretly, she sometimes wondered at the way proverbs contradicted one another. Which was it—the feather makes the jay, or never judge a book by its cover? As she was not, deep down, very scientifically minded, it was all about proving a point. Doctors and lawyers shared the same culture and the same opinions, with biology as the governing law. Race wrote the law, and law determined race...Or maybe it was the other way around, but it made no difference, for nature makes no mistakes; it is the secret of all living things, and everything is based on biology. Belief in nature was confirmed by all that was visible.

Lucie believed that everyone in Europe had the same fundamental ideals, French and German alike. When Friedrich, on a visit to the Burgundy home of his beloved, demonstrated—with the consent of the teachers and the help of a farmer—to the local elementary school pupils how to harvest and thresh wheat, he won over the entire village. "Friedrich is so down-to-earth!" everyone agreed.

Lucie liked the theory of social Darwinism, for she knew all too well that life is a struggle and vices are hereditary. She had seen it as a child, among the cows and the chickens. Once she'd been shown a five-legged calf in a meadow, its extra limb attached like a tail to the animal's back. Another genetic anomaly. What was the point of letting the calf live? It served no purpose, even to itself. Its extra tail couldn't be blamed on the social or family environment. A calf is a calf.

In general terms, the fight was against antisocial elements. There were quite enough alcoholics and idlers. Lucie liked the term *asocial*: a society made up of individuals was untenable; the only thing that counted was the group—as long as it was homogeneous, of course.

As a native of Alsace, Friedrich risked being drafted into the German Army. He had no desire to fight—not, he claimed, out of cowardice, but because he wanted to devote all his energy to his research. He believed that some are born to die immediately after birth, some to die in combat, and some to conceive of a new way of life. *Jedem das Seine*. To each his own role. The terrain of his experiments was not the battlefield. So, unconcerned by the inconsistency, Friedrich gave his family in Alsace a different postal address, so they wouldn't find out he was living in Paris.

His relationship with his family was strained. He did not get on with his father, an industrialist who ran a large cotton mill that produced printed fabric, a business that had been handed down from father to son since the eighteenth century. Having rejected his bourgeois upbringing, Friedrich was passed over by his father in favor of his brother, who had studied applied arts and was being groomed to take over the family business. His sister, three years his junior, also was planning to move to Paris. She shared Friedrich's ideology.

Having recently left the female Hitler Youth, where she had been in the oldest age group of the Band of German Maidens, she had joined the *Nationalsozialistische Volkswohlfahrt*—the National Socialists People's Welfare organization—where she worked as an ancillary nurse. She was proud of her uniform, with its white headdress, large spotless double-breasted apron, and armband. She looked like a secular nun. In the Mulhouse clinic where she worked, the walls were covered in a bright red fabric to make the quotes from *Mein Kampf* stand out. She felt useful and at home there.

Lucie and her sister-in-law hit it off right away the first time they met, though they looked like opposites. Lucie's sister-in-law was a plump, dimpled, innocent young woman, a true blond whose thick complicated German braids, those of a real *Fräulein*, indicated her deep-rooted origins. It had nothing do with being attractive and everything to do with race.

Lucie, by contrast, was worldly-wise and almost too thin. "I don't have time to eat," she declared proudly. She practiced control over her body. The only thing the two women had in common was their fanaticism.

Friedrich was busy with his research in the laboratory and completing his doctoral thesis. He was very rigid, and everyone, including his sister and Lucie, had to defer to him. When he was not working, Friedrich cycled around Paris to meet up with various friends. Lucie was not used to sitting at home waiting for a man to return, but now she had found a man she could not resist. Up until then, it had always been she who kept her man waiting.

One thing Friedrich and Lucie had in common was a complete lack of a sense of humor, something of a National Socialist trait. Their relationship was passionate, intense, and *todernst*—deadly earnest. At twenty-one, Lucie had, in her friends' words, been around the block a few times, but this time she embarked on the relationship as if she had joined a religious order. It was a veritable initiation. Friedrich's vision of the world was total and all-encompassing; Lucie was borne aloft, transported, body and soul. It was to be her vocation for the rest of her life. Was it out of conviction, out of loyalty to Friedrich's memory, out of fear that she had been radically deluded—Lucie persisted in ignoring doubt—or out of a genuine hope of a revival of fascism? Probably all these reasons at once.

Giving in to her father's pressure, the couple decided to marry. It was a small wedding. They had so much else to do. One thing was sure: It had no significance for them. They had no need for fine words or certificates. The whole of Lucie's family, along with Friedrich's sister and brother, came to the civil ceremony. Lucie was marrying into her husband's family; his siblings became for her a substitute family. The ceremony was followed by an excellent black market lunch. They did not invite any friends. Not that they really had any; life was too serious and they were so self-sufficient that Lucie had lost touch with her closest friend from high school, who had introduced her to Friedrich.

Photographs from the wedding day show them posing on the balcony of their new apartment on the Place des

Pyramides. Could there be a more beautiful beginning? There was no religion for these believers in National Socialism. On a late December day in 1941, the slender Lucie wears a pretty, dark woolen wedding dress she made herself, with a high neck and padded shoulders in the fashion of the times. Her small, pert breasts emphasize her gamine look. The nuptials, the absolute antithesis of a white wedding, were absolutely in their image. Lucie is smiling to herself, with an opaque, Madonna-like expression. Friedrich veils his emotions with a slightly horsey smile. He too is looking away from the camera. Of course, they would need to have children, but not immediately. They would wait until they had finished their studies.

Friedrich had been pursued for years by a Benedictine monk he had met in Alsace, back when he was involved, good idealist that he was, in a European youth camp in the Vosges region of France. The camp leaders, as if in anticipation of the coming National Socialism, organized nighttime bonfires, with military-style salutes, singing, and displays of flags.

Dom Germain—a monastic title of Germanic Master, you couldn't have made it up—fancied himself as a mentor of ethics, National Socialist style. He was madly in love with Friedrich. He was lean, clean-shaven, tonsured, humorless, and verbose. When he wasn't hanging around Friedrich on some pretext or other, he was on retreat in a Florentine monastery—Germany and Italy were allies after all—or taking a trip somewhere on the peninsula to learn more about Italian art. Friedrich rebuffed Dom Germain's advances but maintained the friendship, and the monk was determined to organize a religious blessing for the young couple.

I have a recollection of my father, Charles, stealthily slipping a wad of notes to the monk at the end of one of the many family dinners the cleric attended, to bankroll yet another of his "trips to Italy." That evening, Dom Germain, waving his arms around like a gremlin, had monopolized the conversation, forgotten to eat, and made the meal drag on forever. Guffawing, he slapped his thighs with his enormous bony hands. He said unkind things about nuns and church ladies. He didn't smile so much as grimace. Only my mother, her expression bright and eager, listened to what he said. He had the face of an ascetic, with bulging, washed-out blue eyes; he cultivated the look of a holy man. I thought he was like a character from a Bergman movie: Max von Sydow in *The Seventh Seal*.

My father's offering was a sort of thank-you for services rendered, as if he were paying for a psychiatric consultation: Who else could Lucie talk to about National Socialism and the Occupation if not a man of the cloth, homosexual or otherwise, who was committed to the cause and bound by secrecy? My father, who tolerated him for an occasional evening at his table, knew; in a way, he was paying a piece of silver for the monk's services. He must have seen Dom Germain as a kind of safety valve for my mother: for one evening, "our Friedrich" was back, seated with her at dinner.

The monk's presence, a glance, an allusion, had to suffice to alleviate Lucie's pain.

Whenever he went off on one of his trips to Italy, almost always financed by my father, Dom Germain sent us postcards with tormented, homoerotic significance: a Saint Sebastian pierced by innumerable arrows, a plump-buttocked Michelangelo, visions of the apocalypse accompanied by lengthy, excessively punctuated messages in his beautiful handwriting.

After Friedrich's death, and until his own, Dom Germain clung to Lucie and her new family to a degree that was almost indecent. He too had lost the love of his life. He worshiped Friedrich, the hero who died too young, to the end of his days, and made no effort at all to help the young widow move on, even long after she had remarried.

Lucie and Friedrich's ambition was nothing less than to conquer the world—biologically, that is. And if they were to accomplish that, there was work to be done. Radicalism is no laughing matter. Lucie thought of herself more like Clara Petacci, Il Duce's paramour, than Eva Braun, the Führer's mistress, who was a little too self-effacing and submissive for her taste. Lucie adhered to, studied, and embraced Friedrich's radical ideas, absorbing them until they became her own. It was never enough. She was a quick learner, but Friedrich was quicker. He was always one step ahead, and as their relationship grew more intense, Lucie feared that Friedrich would outstrip her. She kept a close eye on him. He was a law unto himself.

Their letters to each other are fascinating. Friedrich's are filled with *Sturm und Drang*, dramatic and enthusiastic accounts of what he's been reading and his latest experiments on rodents. He had his "lesser mice" (female) and his "superior mice" (male). The females were used for the Zondek test—Friedrich avoided uttering the Jewish name out loud—the original pregnancy test: they were injected with the urine of a pregnant woman, then dissected to see if they showed follicular maturation. Friedrich was not the type to take a mistress. His mistresses were his mice, and he was more interested in euthanasia, mitosis and meiosis, dissection, and follicles than sweet talk; duty had summoned him to a higher cause, the romance of science. As far as he was concerned, mice, rats, and Jews were basically the same. In one letter he describes with ghastly relish the twin rodents he is currently working on, how he is priming them for experimentation, demonstration, and the afterlife.

Friedrich found in Lucie a most faithful companion, and she had fallen head over heels in love with him. She was no longer the giddy young woman she had been when they met. Life was a very serious matter: They dreamed of nothing less than the total transformation of France. The actions of the National Socialists were moral because they were political. Any blunders the Nazis made were not crimes; tasks and missions may occasionally have been problematic, but they were always necessary. It was vital to rise above such concerns and keep moving toward perfection. They had to follow the example of the greats. Lucie had been waiting for someone like Friedrich to come along, for French fascism to meet German fascism. At last science was at the service of the state; at last ideas had found a way of transforming society. The future was theirs. Lucie had met fanatics before, but never for a cause so far-reaching and concrete. Theirs was a union as ideological as it was romantic.

In their spare time the couple went hiking in the high mountains, with ice axes and heavy boots, to contemplate the snow line. Lucie hated this, but she gritted her teeth and put up with it.

Their mission in life was messianic; their task was to educate the French to embrace National Socialism. The people were not to be left to think for themselves; they had to be helped to understand.

The couple's apartment had been provided by the Commissariat-General for Jewish Affairs, which noted that the previous tenant—a Jew—had "departed." The apartment was declared vacant for a just and true cause. Lucie and Friedrich took it over for a piddling rent. Fate smiled on the couple. Friedrich was making good progress in his research and now had only to complete his thesis. Lucie was in the last year of her double degree. They had friends in high places. They were renting an apartment for next to nothing. They were young and the future belonged to them. They suffered no guilty conscience: Jews, no better than laboratory mice, did not deserve to live on the Place des Pyramides next to the Louvre. Lucie and Friedrich's ambition, in line with their Nazi convictions, was not to become materially rich—money, an instrument of capitalism, was of no interest to them—but to ensure that their world would come to be. Nazism was their version of the Napoleonic ideal of the Battle of the Nations.

Friedrich was an intellectual and an idealist, though he loathed such labels: he thought intellectuals were lazy and idealists ought to focus on action. He was aware of the spectacular progress in human genetics being made by the team led by Dr. Otmar von Verschür at the Berlin Institute of Anthropology. (It was Verschür who suggested to one of his colleagues, Dr. Mengele, that he ask to be posted to one of the concentration camps run by the German General Governorate for the Occupied Polish Region, to further his research on living subjects. In 1943 Mengele sent Verschür some interesting analyses of his experiments on twins and other human specimens at Auschwitz.)

Friedrich, convinced of the neutrality (human tissue is human tissue, after all) of medical histology, was an avid follower of Verschür's research. Verschür's *Manual of Eugenics and Human Heredity* had recently been published in French, translated by Friedrich's friend George Montandon, although the book's German title, *Rassenhygiene*, was simpler and more to the point. The book explained certain hereditary predispositions and their consequences. It all made absolute sense. It was clear that everything was bound up with everything else.

Friedrich was a true romantic, with a deep love of literature. He worshiped Louis Ferdinand Auguste Destouches, better known by his pen name, Louis-Ferdinand Céline, author of *Journey to the End of the Night*. Destouches was a medical doctor as well as a writer, obsessed by race and decadence, with a profound hatred for Jews. Indeed he seemed to have held almost everything and everyone in contempt; the only things he cared for were his cats and his wife. When his notorious antisemitic pamphlet *Bagatelles for a Massacre* was republished in 1941 (it went on to become one of the bestsellers of the Occupation), he gave Friedrich a signed copy. Until she died, Lucie kept the book by her bedside in the house in Burgundy, along with a copy of Marcel Proust's *Albertine Gone*, the sixth volume of *In Search of Lost Time*. Proust was Jewish, of course, but like Céline he had an exceptional style.

Friedrich gave up smoking after the wedding and for every packet of cigarettes he didn't smoke he bought himself a new tome. He always seemed to have a book in his hand.

Céline didn't often leave his house, but occasionally he and his wife would cycle from Montmartre to the center of Paris, where they would meet up with friends and attend lectures at the *Institut d'étude des questions juives*, the Institute for the Study of Jewish Affairs, set up by the Gestapo—people tended to simply say "the Germans"—in the wake of the establishment of the Commissariat-General for Jewish Affairs. It was situated at 21 Rue la Boétie, in the building that had once housed Paul Rosenberg's famous gallery; now, instead of displaying Impressionist and Cubist paintings, the institute served as a site for discussion of the so-called Jewish question (which at the time had yet to find its final solution).

The institute served both as a sort of unofficial embassy and as a laboratory for a particularly French style of antisemitism and propaganda.

Friedrich, Lucie, Céline, and Céline's wife, Lucette, regularly met up at the French Institute, along with the two Karls from the German Institute, which was attached to the embassy. Karl Epting was the cultural adviser who had introduced Céline's work to a German readership, and his deputy, the historian Karl (Heinz) Bremer, a close friend of Friedrich's, was head of literary translation.

When Friedrich hadn't seen Céline in a while, he liked to cycle up to Montmartre, where Céline and Lucette lived with their cat Bébert. He loved visiting this peaceful haven to talk with his mentor and listen to him grousing about the Jews.

Several years later, long after Friedrich's death, my mother, now remarried, sent me to school in the Paris suburb of Meudon. One of my father's colleagues had recommended an *école nouvelle*, a school based on a new philosophy of education. The school had adopted the principles of Vichy pedagogy; even the typewriters in the secretary's office, with their special font, were the very ones that had been used during the Occupation. The school was located a few minutes' walk from the house where Céline and his wife Lucette moved to in 1951. Whenever Lucie took me to school in her rattletrap of a 2CV, as we drove up the Route des Gardes and past their street, she would invariably glance down it toward the house where the couple lived until his death, and where his widow remained until she died in 2019, aged 107. When I was born, my mother named me Coline, not daring to go any further, but oddly enough I am often called Céline by strangers, as if they can see right through to my mother's most secret wish.

Naturally, Friedrich drew up a long list of books for Lucie to read. First, Jacques Benoist-Méchin's *An Explanation of Mein Kampf*, a classic, its cover embossed with a gilded swastika. Then came volumes on law, science, and politics, which, Friedrich explained, expounded the same core ideas. He gave Lucie *How to Recognize a Jew?* by the aforementioned George Montandon. Montandon, a Swiss French anthropologist who specialized in "ethno-racial science," was chair of the Ethnic Commission (just a couple letters away from an Ethics Commission) of the far-right Parti Populaire Français.

The PPF, founded and headed by Jacques Doriot, was a fascist and collaborationist political party whose ideology was founded on the science of racism, both general and specifically Jewish ethno-racism. It was headquartered in Paris, at 10 Rue des Pyramides, a stone's throw from the square where Lucie and Friedrich lived. This was where Friedrich's band of ideological sympathizers regularly met up, and sometimes the great man Jacques himself came by to greet them. Lucie found in Doriot the moral fiber and smooth-tongued eloquence necessary to awaken the French from their torpor and persuade them to follow his ideology.

Lucie and Friedrich were also involved with the antisemitic periodical *Le Cahier Jaune* (The Yellow Notebook), and the children's magazine *Youpino*, both published by the Commissariat-General for Jewish Affairs.

When I was a child, I found some bright yellow pamphlets in the Burgundy house, filled with black drawings of ghoulish faces and seven-branched candelabras. The headline banners were unfathomable: "They are striking at our literature." "Don't mention Jewification." There was a special full-color issue, entitled *Je vous hais* ("I hate you"), illustrated with a face whose mouth was a huge gaping hole. This must have been the last of the series, because it was not in the customary *Cahier* format. We had a game at home called *Yellow Dwarf*, but I didn't understand why a yellow pamphlet would be so literally entitled *Le Cahier Jaune*. It was not until years later that I discovered that yellow has long been the color assigned to Jews; it was the color of the roundel, the little piece of fabric Jews were made to wear in the Middle Ages, as well, of course, of the yellow star they were forced to wear under the Nazis. A yellow book for the "yellow" people, *J* for *jaune*, and implicitly for the Jews; like the *Code Noir*, the Black Code, written under Louis XIV and designed to govern every aspect of the lives of enslaved and free African people under French colonial rule.

Alongside her biology and law studies, Lucie was working on an exhibition, "The Jew and France," to take place in Paris in the summer of 1941. She had been recommended to the propaganda service by her uncle Gaston to help with picture research and captions.

The mandate was clear: The exhibition was an adaptation of German propaganda, but this must not be apparent. The aim was to demonstrate, from a specifically French angle, that "the Jew" was always an interloper acting against the country's interests.

There was panel after panel of "proof," corroborated with figures and graphs. But it was the photographs of the guilty that every visitor came to see.

Lucie's job was to select portraits to illustrate each theme. About ten photographs were required for each panel, with the face cut out and the name handwritten alongside.

Who should personify "Lies," "Monopolies," and "Mind Control?" It was not so much a display as a litany. Lucie had no equal when it came to picking out sneering, sinister faces. After exhausting the press archives, she combed through the propaganda collection and documents in the anthropometric service of the Prefecture of Police. The result was very effective: an alarming community was threatening the French.

Lucie was pleased with her work. Initially, Uncle Gaston gave her guidance. It was easy for him, with his experience of laying out the front pages of *Paris-Soir*. A headline is supposed take a second and a half to read, the eye zigzagging from left to right. Important text should always be positioned on the right-hand side of the panel.

Lucie was bright and caught on quickly. The exhibition was a huge success. Thousands of visitors crowded into the Palais Berlitz. She was not credited in the exhibition catalogue, but everyone at the propaganda service knew of her involvement. Abetz, the Reich ambassador to occupied France, asked to meet the team. Lucie accepted an invitation to a cocktail party at the embassy on Rue de Lille, one of collaborationist Paris's high-society hubs. She cycled there across the Seine.

In the Salon d'Honneur, surrounded by a throng of young officers trying to speak French and airmen in white spencer jackets, Ambassador Abetz looked rather laid-back in his dark suit. He congratulated the capable young woman on her contribution to the exhibition, which had clearly found its audience. He spoke excellent, if heavily accented, French. Lucie listened, politely inclining her head. He must have been about fifteen years her senior. The young woman sensed the young man in Abetz: serious, not very endearing, but tenacious. He still had something of the country bumpkin about him. And the ambassador recognized in Lucie the little country girl she had once been.

Abetz talked to her about "cultural collaboration" and the social advances of the new Germany. "Propaganda is our Trojan horse. Your newspapers must speak out in favor of our collaboration. For propaganda to be effective it must be targeted. It is up to the French themselves to give their backing to the dissemination of German culture in France."

Lucie listened attentively. He was a good talker. And she had always been a good listener.

She slipped away without having drunk even one glass of champagne. The evening had been a modest success.

When, toward the end of October 1941, Uncle Gaston learned that anyone running a poster campaign now had to apply for a permit, he gained admittance for Lucie, with general approval, to the *Oraff*, the office responsible for poster design and distribution. Lucie was no longer a nobody. Though the organization appeared to be French, it was in fact run by the Germans. Goebbels's instructions were strict: no publication without official endorsement. Gaston knew how difficult it was to obtain the famous stamp of approval.

The activities of the propaganda service were wide-ranging and apparently contradictory, combining censorship, information, and propaganda in a single department. Its directives were exacting. At *Oraff*, Lucie was to create "French" posters while working within the guidelines established by the propaganda service. It was a job for an interpreter: creating French slogans out of German documentation. Fortunately, she spoke the language well and her slogans were lively. Where did she get her ideas from? They were anti-Bolshevik, anti-Masonic, anti-Jewish, anti-English—anti-everything—and all her posters were accepted. She had an excellent instinct for what would and would not fly.

Uncle Gaston could always spot her style, a mixture of impudence and bad faith, a glib way with words, a way of twisting things to mean their opposite. She was a collaborationist Rosie the Riveter, with a cheeky stance that she got from the proletariat side of the family.

Whatever it was, it worked. She swiftly made her way

up the ladder, until she was designing posters of all sizes and pamphlets. All of it, officially, French.

The *Oraff* office was located in an imposing Haussmann-era building at the top end of the Champs-Élysées, number 138, on the right-hand side not far from the Arc de Triomphe, the "right" side of the Champs-Élysées, the side that got the sunshine, near the propaganda service office. Everyone knew it. Between the two buildings was the Radio Paris studio.

She sometimes crossed the river to the Left Bank for meetings with Abetz's staff, but she had little interest in socializing. There was too much to be done.

The Germans in Paris couldn't get enough of "Luzie." She became known as the Leni Riefenstahl of the poster. Quite the honor. She pulled out all the stops in her efforts to merit the comparison with Riefenstahl, one of the Führer's intimates. Leni and Luzie!

Uncle Gaston introduced her to Philippe Henriot, the French journalist, politician, and Nazi collaborator who served as a minister in the French government at Vichy, for whom he directed propaganda broadcasts. He was one of the best-known figures in collaborationist Parisian high society.

Henriot, with his broad smile, and Lucie, with her impish expression and lively eyes, first met on Rue de Lille. They were both, in a way, in the same line of work, though Lucie worked in the shadows, and Henriot was very much in the spotlight. She was impressed by his stature, in the literal sense of the term. He had the virile air of a man who had to shave twice a day. Henriot, a charmer and a connoisseur, quoted some of Lucie's slogans back to her: "Every fib flies out of the same nest," illustrated by a flock of Capitoline geese flying in formation over England. "Workers, you have the key to the camps," was used to explain *Opération Relève*, in which one prisoner of war was released and sent back to France for every three French workers sent to do forced labor in Germany. Lucie was not only helping the French understand the situation, she was also sounding the alarm.

In response, Lucie recalled Henriot's prewar political engagement, when he opposed the parliamentary system and was already warning of the dangers of the Republic. She addressed him as Monsieur, he called her "my dear little Lucie," and they danced around each other in an enchanting little game of verbal ping-pong.

The Germans nicknamed Lucie *die Propagandistin*, the propagandist. With her no-nonsense attitude and unwavering set of priorities, she seemed to be everywhere at once.

It was a great stroke of luck to meet someone as influential as Henriot—for the clan, for Vichy, for the Third Reich. If there were two or three other figures like him, more of the weak and the cowardly would have soon switched sides. He was on first-name terms with Abetz. Friedrich Grimm, the ambassador's private secretary, nicknamed him the French Goebbels. Even Ribbentrop wanted to meet him.

After Henriot was assassinated by the Resistance in 1944, Lucie came up with a simple but punchy slogan: "He told the Truth... They murdered him for it!" She was loyal to the end.

For four years, Lucie blossomed in her work. When she was out of ideas for her posters, she popped into the offices of *Signal* to lend a hand. In all, two million copies of the magazine were distributed in twenty-five languages, eight hundred thousand of them in French.

As in other occupied countries, *Signal* was Germany's point of reference in France, its propaganda showpiece. Its editors were recruited for their knowledge of the target country. Lucie was sometimes consulted for her opinion. Her answers were pithy and to the point. She was often to be found leaning over a light table peering at photographic contact sheets through a magnifying glass. She was partially responsible for the *Rural* and *Daily Life* sections of the magazine, contributing photographic portraits of mustachioed old French winegrowers in berets, their expressions debonair and wily, and features on insouciant young women who epitomized carefree French style. Even her own family wanted to be featured. Lucie disapproved but let it go. Of course, they were never named.

Every so often Lucie dropped into the French broadcasting service on Rue François-Premier, a stone's throw from the Champs-Élysées, to work on *actualités mondiales*, propaganda newsreels adapted from German newsreels and screened in movie theaters before the main feature. Sometimes they covered events in France. Lucie would be asked her opinion on a particular story, which was then edited and dubbed in Berlin.

It was at Lucie's suggestion that the meeting between Maréchal Pétain and Reichsmarschall Göring on December

1st, 1941, took place at the railway station in the Burgundy village of Saint-Florentin. The purpose of the meeting was to discuss the *Burgund* Project, the establishment of the Order-State of Burgundy—a plan, dear to Lucie's heart, for a Teutonic version of the ancient Burgundian kingdom of Lotharingia. Everything was meticulously prepared, and Marshal Pétain was provided with detailed notes on the plan. The two leaders enjoyed an excellent lunch of local Burgundy specialties in Göring's armored carriage. Lucie accompanied the film crew and stood behind the camera.

The newsreel shows the official carriages taking a wide curve, then slowing down as the train passes through the village of Les Chomettes, Lucie's birthplace, a few kilometers from Saint-Florentin. Only the propagandist could have devised such a route.

But the meeting was not a success and was cut short. The French were trying to impress, which displeased the occupying forces. Göring turned to Pétain at the end of the meeting and asked him, haughtily, "Who won the war, you or us?" It was the last anyone was to hear of the *Burgund* Project.

At the end of a long working day, Lucie returned to the apartment she shared with Friedrich. He questioned her about her work, her studies, her reading. Lucie was studying law, but studying law on its own made no sense; since law was, in essence, biology, she had to continue with biology. Eventually, at the heart of the Thousand-Year Reich, there would be those who had studied biology, the superior beings, and the rest. So, on top of her professional activities, Lucie doggedly carried on studying both law and biology. Once she had her double degree she would be able to work alongside Friedrich. "It's only right that I should expect you to help me realize my full potential," he wrote to her with typical pomposity. Some evenings she could barely stay awake as Friedrich droned on ("Lucie, are you listening?" Eyes closed, she nodded her head, "Yes, I'm listening."). Her law examinations were coming up—she still had to bone up on administrative and civil law, privacy, and bank loans. There was her final biology examination in October to prepare for. Friedrich's reading list. Not to mention her propaganda work. Life was indeed a most serious matter.

Lucie did not have a scientific mind, and she struggled to retain the basics in biology, particularly the theory of germplasm. What a word! It sounded like a translation. As far as she understood, it was something to do with genetic resources, about distinguishing innate and acquired traits, separating the soma from the germ. Germ cells pass from one generation to the next and are not influenced by any life experience. Cells that were racial. Racialized cells, as it were. Lucie's favorite example was mice. No matter how many generations of rodents have their tails cut off, their babies are always born with long tails. Their germ cells are unchanged, thus proving the constant nature of the germplasm. Same as with the Jews. Whatever they did, they would always be Jews. It made perfect sense to Lucie.

Friedrich bred rodents in the laboratory but refused to bring any back to the apartment. A mouse is not a pet. Lucie disliked all animals, but Friedrich's mice were an applied example of germplasm, and she liked things that were concrete. She marveled at the term, as she did at the term *seminal fluid*, a "healthy biological substance produced in large quantities." Such a convoluted formulation for something so tangible.

When I was in middle school, in the 1970s, my mother made me recite germplasm theory, which was on the biology syllabus for my science *baccalauréat*. I got everything mixed up.

But Lucie could never remember the term *DNA*, also on my biology syllabus, no doubt because DNA is proof of scientific rationality. She was still thinking in terms of dominant and recessive genes, which was how she understood the world.

What she really enjoyed was making things with her hands. She loved to sew and paint. She was very practical, good with her hands, and even built the odd piece of furniture. I have a photograph taken by Friedrich showing Lucie and her sister-in-law bent over their work, wry little smiles hinting at their closeness.

Every evening, Friedrich pored over his heavy volumes of anatomical pathology. Lucie occasionally leafed through them too. It was almost unbelievable what degeneration could lead to. And as for all those recessive genes...

When I was a little girl, I found a shelf of Friedrich's medical textbooks on the upper floor of the house in Les Chomettes.

It was almost as if he were about to return and take up his studies again. I pulled out a book by the forgotten biologist Heinz Graupner, whose specialty was aquatic invertebrates. According to the dog-eared copy of *Hormones and Vitamins*, Graupner prescribed elixirs of life for women and counseled men on daily hygiene. Then a heavy leather-bound, lavishly illustrated volume caught my eye. It contained descriptions of different human pathologies, which all seemed, bizarrely, to have a sexual connotation. Fascinated and horrified, I leafed through the pages. Elephantiasis. The picture showed a man—a "savage"—half naked, clad in only a loincloth, transporting his monstrous equipment on a wheelbarrow. His genitalia were so much bigger than an elephant's that he looked like he was struggling to lift the shaft. Syphilitic canker of the tongue, advanced stage. The sight of the canker devouring the tissue was revolting. Supernumerary breasts: a perfectly round breast growing between the two shoulder blades of a woman whose face was partially hidden. Conjoined twins, attached at the head and the back.

It was a textbook of abnormalities. The patients were monsters. Rather than providing medical information, the catalogue seemed like a clarion call for euthanasia. I closed the book, deeply disturbed. I would never, ever study medicine.

Lucie was in love. Fantasizing about her future with Friedrich, she decided, "If I am to follow him, I will have to adopt his opinions." All the reading and studying she did was for him. "I cannot wait to see you," she wrote to him, "and snuggle together under the covers." They were constantly writing to each other, even during the briefest absence. Lucie's letters were lyrical: "There is a hill here, with a field of cornflowers at the top, and a cool breeze. Oh, Friedrich, that breeze . . ." She didn't finish the sentence.

Friedrich was more German than the Germans, more Nazi than the Nazis. "We simply have to get rid of the Jews," he wrote to his young wife. They were not to waver. Once people began getting picked off, not many would be left, but they didn't worry about that. They were young; they would be around for a thousand years. Forever.

I once caught my mother sitting in a corner of a room on the first floor of the house in Burgundy, engrossed in reading her correspondence with Friedrich. She lifted her head when she heard me. Her chignon had fallen loose; her face was drawn. She was clutching a bundle of letters whose pale blue ink was blotted with tears. She wiped her nose with the back of her hand and choked back a sob. She couldn't speak. I was shocked. Now I knew for sure: Lucie had secrets from a former life.

Years later, Lucie gave me the letters. Hers were written in beautiful copperplate. Some were hard to decipher in places. When I became a historian, I began looking at them more closely, even though I was frightened to intrude on their intimacy. So much sensuality and lunacy, as if every shred of good sense had been scrambled by ideology. On June 25th, 1944, Friedrich wrote to his wife: "Year 28 of my birth, year 1,000 of our love." Time itself was accelerating.

They had four years of glory and passion. But despite the best efforts of the propagandist, the German army was routed and Paris was liberated in August 1944. Harsh reality began to catch up with Lucie and Friedrich. Friedrich continued going to the laboratory as if nothing were amiss. The posterior pituitary was disappointing, but one interesting hypothesis seemed to have been confirmed. Truth would triumph.

But the winds were changing. A few weeks after the Liberation, a gloomy Friedrich arrived home one evening and announced he had decided to throw in his lot with the Americans. His intention was not to change sides, merely to appear as if he were. Altering various key details of his life and work, he was going to offer his services to the Americans—he could not bring himself to utter the word *Allies*—as a medical student in Paris who had grown up in Alsace, and thus spoke German fluently. He could work as a translator and an informant.

He had been changing sides, in a way, his whole life, with Alsace regularly relocated from one side of the border to the other. He had originally left home to avoid conscription. Now he was going to go one step further. He had heard about a large air base in the town of Beaumont-le-Roger, in the Eure department, formerly German, and now under American control. He told Lucie he was going to cycle to Normandy to replenish supplies; when he got there he would inveigle an introduction to the American camp commander.

For the first time in their relationship, Lucie was unpersuaded. Given Friedrich's Nazi sympathies, the idea that the Americans would accept his services as an intelligence agent didn't hold water for a second. He had never been part of any Resistance network. Did he take the Americans for fools? The fate of turncoats was well-known: the previous spring, when Vichy's former interior minister Pierre Pucheu had gone to see General de Gaulle in Algiers, he was sentenced to death and executed by firing squad.

Friedrich was adamant, leading to a furious fight with Lucie. He was feeling hunted, like a laboratory mouse. Was it because of the assassination, a few weeks earlier, of his friend and mentor Montandon, inventor of the perfect taxonomy? A band of "terrorists"—the bastards!—had shot him at his home in Clamart, near Paris.

Lucie was terrified of losing Friedrich; she couldn't bear that he wouldn't listen to her. In the end, fed up and having run out of arguments, weeping tears of rage, she cried, "If that's the way it is, do what you want, and die!"

It was October 3rd, 1944, the day before Lucie's birthday. Friedrich walked out of the house and slammed the front door behind him. She never saw him again.

He died. Too suspicious, too implicated, too recognizable, still taking risks and refusing to face reality.

The American authorities delivered his body to Lucie four days later. She went to Normandy to identify him. A death certificate was drawn up. The carpenter from the nearby village of Le Plessis made the coffin and cosigned the death certificate as both bailiff and gravedigger. Friedrich was buried in the village cemetery, near the boundary wall, beneath a simple mound of earth. The casket was placed directly in the ground. What epitaph should she give him? *Für Führer, Volk, und Vaterland*? For the Führer, the People, the Fatherland? Which Fatherland? In the end there was nothing—no gravestone, no name, no date. She put up a simple, outsized cross. It was enough. It covered a multitude of sins. But if you looked closely, it was quite clearly an iron cross.

Lucie left Friedrich's body buried at this remote spot. She maintained the lease on the plot for the rest of her life, and she often came to weep at his grave, which she kept there, for herself, despite the requests of Friedrich's family that his body be sent home to Alsace.

To anyone who dared ask the cause of Friedrich's death, she always began with the same words: "He was walking down Rue d'Aboukir," and then she would stop, overwhelmed by grief. But Rue d'Aboukir, which led to the offices of *Signal* magazine, was a long way from Normandy.

The gynaeceum pitied her. Sometimes it really seemed as if Lucie were losing her mind.

When I pressed her, she gave me different versions. Once she told me Friedrich had been cycling the wrong way down a one-way street; he didn't see the American tank coming in the other direction and was run over. I didn't understand how you could die from going the "wrong way." Another time she told me he'd "dropped dead." I had no idea what that could mean. Had he been dropped to his death?

One day I poked my head into the gynaeceum, and out of Lucie's earshot, I heard someone whisper, "All these stories. None of it makes any sense." But when she saw the others' expressions, she didn't dare go on.

Friedrich was a constant presence throughout my childhood. He was always there, dead and alive, absent and present. Even my father tolerated him, and he ended up granting Friedrich a space in our lives.

Alone with her ghosts, Lucie spent the rest of her life—sixty-two years—devoted to the memory of her great love, preciously guarding the image of the life and mission that might have been theirs had the French not been, as she saw it, such cowards—if they had been more idealistic, if they had turned out in greater numbers to fight alongside the Germans. Her last exchange with her husband played over and over in her head. "I know how Friedrich died," was her tacit, unfathomable message.

There was no more talk of law or biology. She married again and had four children. It was halfhearted. She had already lived her life. She would always remain resolutely faithful to Friedrich's memory.

Friedrich never told his story. Lucie never would.

On the surface, Lucie returned to more orthodox pursuits. Charles, her second husband, who asked no questions and in whom she confided nothing, was an altar boy compared to those who had preceded him. He remained a loyal Pétainist right up to the end of his life—though he opportunistically joined the Resistance in the weeks leading up to the Liberation—but nevertheless had showed great courage during the D-Day landings and the Alsace campaign. His very French-style antisemitism was that of a right-wing Catholic nationalist who saw Jews as overly careerist and ambitious, a problem to be solved, needing to be taught a lesson.

Charles was directly involved in the modernization of postwar France. It was the heyday of economic growth. He had a successful career as a senior civil servant: after the École Nationale d'Administration, the newly established institute for training high-ranking civil servants, he worked at the Cour des Comptes, the French national audit office, became chief of staff at the War Ministry, then went on to become a senior executive at a large oil company. An eternal number two, both professionally and in his marriage.

In a way, Charles and Lucie were made for each other. They formed an alliance. Like Lucie, Charles was a great reader, but he didn't read Proust, André Schwarz-Bart, Romain Gary, or Joseph Kessel. He collected books like the beautiful leather-bound Pléiade edition of the writings of the aristocrat and anthropologist Arthur de Gobineau, who developed the theory of the Aryan master race.

I still had no answers to my questions.

3

By October 1944, the total accounting of their collaboration was bleak: Friedrich was dead and Lucie, a widow at the age of just twenty-five, who had lost her job and had barely any friends, was jumpy and anxious. Not only was she dealing with grief and depression, she also had to face a future that was likely to involve going underground to avoid the humiliation of having her head shaved as a collaborator, being put on trial, or simply being shot dead on a street corner by the new rulers of Paris.

After she met Friedrich in 1940 she was extremely happy, but now her mood was increasingly unstable, and for the rest of her life she alternated between periods of depression and manic self-confidence. Nothing, no matter how hard she tried to put on a brave face, more for herself than anyone else, was as it used to be. She lost both her convictions and her vitality, as if she had adopted a new motto, expressing both bravado and fatalism: "*Même pas peur, même pas mal!*" (I'm not scared, you can't hurt me!). She, who took such great care not to be unmasked, no longer bothered to lock the front door. Inside, outside, what difference did it make? What was the worst that could happen after all that had already happened? What could all the thieves in the world take from her, now that she had lost everything? The front door of the house in Les Chomettes was always left unlocked, even at night, in case Friedrich were to steal back in. She never locked the 2CV; indeed she often left the trunk open, a trick that allowed her to park wherever she liked. She used to leave fabric sample catalogues scattered on the back seat to make it look as if she were an interior designer on a site visit. Not that it made much difference, given that a 2CV is so easy to get into anyway. It worked like a charm.

She was constantly losing things and then finding them again, which meant at one point she had three driver's licenses. On the highway she would stop at the toll booth, then realize she had no coins. Everything was flat and dull, she was indifferent to it all, her life was behind her, and she offset her depressions with periods of manic activity.

My mother told me she spent much of 1944 bedridden because of a primary infection that left her with a shadow on her lung. Her condition was nowhere near as serious as that of her closest friend, a medical student whom she said had been at death's door. The young woman had pulmonary tuberculosis and Lucie invited her to convalesce at the family house in Burgundy. For a time, it was as if their two lives merged into one. Lucie no longer really knew who she was, woman or propagandist; she vacillated between her memories of republican France, her National Socialist years, an obsession with passing on those values, and sheer madness.

One thing was sure: Even after she remarried, she was to remain, for the rest of her life, the widow of her first husband, doing her utmost, for over six decades and in a thousand different ways, to keep his memory alive. As guardian of the temple dedicated to her hero, she championed his life and work, even while she kept certain aspects of his life secret. Friedrich would always remain young and spirited, looking toward the future, a poster boy for National Socialism. As he wrote to her on July 7th, 1944: "Know that here on earth, all things eventually pass, except true love." The thing about someone who dies young is that they never grow old. Lucie used to like to quote, almost like a litany, two lines from Gluck's *Orpheus and Euridice*, a popular opera during the Occupation: "I have lost my Eurydice / Nothing can match my misfortune." She quoted Racine too: "In a month, in a year, how much must we suffer, Lord, when so many seas separate me from you?"

She had strange dreams, from which she would awaken the following morning with no idea how old she was, because to remember the date meant remembering that Friedrich was dead. She would ramble on about how he had died the day before her birthday, but which birthday? What year was it? Uncertainty gave her a kind of security. And so, like a good revolutionary, Lucie invented a new calendar: year one was the year she met Friedrich, which meant that 1944 was year four, and it was the four that mattered to her. Lucie was twenty-four in 1944, and now, to find her bearings, she counted in tens from the moment when everything stopped. How old am I this morning? Not twenty-four, of course. Not thirty-four, no. Forty-four? Fifty-four? It barely mattered. She would get confused, try to remember. "I had such a powerful dream," she would say, "that when I woke up, I didn't know anything anymore."

The approximate ages of her children provided some kind of benchmark. By the time Lucie had woken up properly and remembered that Friedrich was dead, she had a semblance of understanding; but, unable to accept it, she would begin reeling off the decades again, as if reciting a mantra to soothe her overwhelming pain.

After all, wasn't it true that in the *Milice*, the paramilitary force of the Vichy regime—in other words, among her collaborationist friends—they counted by hands, in fives, tens, twenties, and thirties? The basic unit was one hand, whose five fingers represented five men, the hand as symbol of fraternity. Then ten: there is literally strength in numbers. Then thirty—the leader of thirty men is a real somebody. Lucie liked leaders: the leader of the hand, leader of ten, leader of thirty, division leader. It was impressive. Every town was gridded, numbered, and barracked. One of Lucie's favorite expressions was easy enough to understand: "All together as one"—behind the leader, of course.

The advantage of this unusual decimal system was that anyone could modify and employ it as they wished. Lucie was so on board with this sequencing concept that when it came to registering us for school, sports clubs, art classes, and so on, she would concoct wholly imaginary dates of birth for each of us. When it came to calculating and remembering, she adapted her usual rule: start in the year four and add a multiple of ten.

This led to her declaring, with all the aplomb she could muster, "No, Madame, my child is not yet eighteen." Or "Yes, Monsieur, my daughter is fourteen. She is still entitled to a child's ticket."

She had four children, which in a way simplified things. She knew that the Nazis had provided economic incentives for Germans with at least four children. So she had it made. She had borne four children for Lotharingen France, four children to serve the Fascist Restoration, or, failing that, to bear witness. And yet on days when she was depressed, she would calculate not in multiples of four but in multiples of ten: "I'm a hundred years old today."

On October 6th, 1944, the day after her birthday, Lucie and her sister-in-law went up to Normandy to identify her husband's body. According to Friedrich's sister's account, Lucie entered the room where the dead man lay. His head was partially wrapped in a bandage. Shaking with sobs, she threw herself on his body, then buried her face in his groin, moaning over and over, "It's mine, it's mine, it's mine." Where was she planning to keep it? She was filled with utter rage and despair. Nothing mattered anymore.

Friedrich was officially declared to have died in Plessis, a village in the Eure department of Normandy located between Évreux and Bernay. According to family lore, he was killed "following an altercation with a Black American." He had gone out on his bicycle to find food; exhausted and finding himself in an area off-limits to civilians, he hitched himself to a U.S. Army truck that had refused him aid. The driver, hoping to shake him off, accelerated sharply and Friedrich was knocked off his bicycle. His skull was crushed by the truck's side rail.

I have found no trace of this accident in the archives. What I do know is that in the weeks leading up to his death, Friedrich met an American army officer called Jeremiah, under somewhat murky circumstances. In civilian life, Jeremiah worked as an engineer in Boston; in the U.S. Army he served as a judge in an American military court. Jeremiah was a naturalized German-born Jewish American, stationed at the large German air base that straddled the villages of Beaumontel and Beaumont-le-Roger, which, as soon as it was liberated by the Allies, was taken over by the Americans. A dozen miles away, at Écaquelon and Bosgouet, were two launchpads for V1 flying bombs—the original cruise missiles.

How did Friedrich come to be there? He appears to have had a couple of old school friends living in the region whom he had contacted back in the summer of 1940, briefly writing on a notepad the names of the towns where they lived, Beaumont and Montfort, but not their names. Had he gone there four years later with the idea of pretending to have access to the secrets of the much-talked-about V2 miracle weapons? It is not inconceivable that he went there with the slightly crazy idea of saving his skin that way; perhaps he thought that cooperating with the enemy would mean he would be left alone and not tried as a collaborator. Only one thing is for sure: he did not die at Le Plessis. His body was taken there after his death.

Jeremiah was certainly not averse to the idea of working with Friedrich, though it is unlikely he knew all there was to know about him; more significantly, he fell completely under Lucie's spell. Now that Friedrich was dead, killed by his army, Jerry, as my mother called him, clearly felt a sense of culpability, and was eager to help Lucie. I think he would have liked to marry her, even though he was already married to a snub-nosed American Episcopalian (allegedly descended from the Pilgrims), with whom he had a child.

Whatever his motive, he found Lucie a paid job in the U.S. Army. It was a dream come true for her: to move seamlessly from the camp of the occupier to that of the liberator, and, moreover, through the intermediary of a Jew. A masterstroke. The young woman simply swapped sides, pulling off what Friedrich had failed to do. Everyone was happy. Jerry felt like he was settling a war debt on behalf of the U.S. Army. Lucie felt like a born-again virgin, working for the winning side, amused by the feelings of guilty responsibility that an American Jew had for a Pétain supporter and widow of a Nazi sympathizer. And Charles, her future husband, was eternally grateful to Jerry, and all the others, for having come to his wife's aid.

Jerry was a bit of a mystery. He was Jewish, but his family history was hard to fathom. Perhaps he had been born in Austria, not Germany. Lucie always wondered if he was ashamed of being Jewish: the way he was fascinated by the Germans, how troubled he had been by meeting Friedrich. She had no one to talk to about any of this. She had gradually built up a group of friends, including members of Friedrich's family, and everyone was so different from everyone else; by this point there had to be a few members of the Resistance involved as well, for the sake of expediency.

An unusual relationship developed between Jerry and Lucie, which was to last all their lives and was passed on from family to family, between France and the United States, Paris and Boston. My sister was named after Jerry's wife, Meredith, an unusual first name in France at the time, a little precious, but with the advantage of concealment; it was even a little disorienting, for even though she had white-blond hair and ice-blue eyes, my parents could hardly have chosen a name more different from Gretchen or Waltraud.

The rest of the family was roped in to strengthen the families' transatlantic alliance; the precautionary laundering of National Socialism had certain requirements. My brother was often sent to stay in Boston. Jerry had an affair with a friend of my mother's—almost like a proxy relationship with Lucie—and Jerry's daughter eventually settled in France.

Incapable of feeling guilt, Lucie wove endless fictions and used other people to her own ends.

Reticent, I kept my distance and didn't allow myself to be impressed by Jerry, a portly, garrulous man who was always either dangling his rectangular tortoiseshell spectacles off the tip of a finger or sucking one of its arms. I couldn't bear his ogre eyebrows, his sparse, slicked-back, gray hair, his unexpectedly nasal accent, his forced bonhomie and adenoidal laugh: he was always trying too hard to seduce me, or, rather, my mother through me.

Whenever he came to visit, he brought beautiful toys and Native American jewelry as gifts. He fixed everything in the apartment and crafted exquisite marquetry boxes. Everyone laughed at his jokes. Lucie and the clan's efforts reaped the most benefits: they had an American, ex-military, and, better still, Jewish family in their entourage. Not one of those boastful types, as Lucie might have put it, but a Jew with a hang-up about being Jewish, the only one to be invited in, as it turned out, who had sullied himself by dodgy dealings with Nazis and their associates. He had all the advantages: he was both extremely Jewish and extremely not Jewish. And then, of course, there was the fact that he had known Friedrich, "my husband—my first husband, that is. Anyway, you must stay for dinner! I've got a lovely rosy piece of beef cooking in the oven," Lucie would exclaim. She loved red meat. She loved the word *red*, whose subtly different allusions she fathomed with both horror and fascination. Black and red, like the Nazi flag. Or rotting meat.

Lucie was fully aware of the debt of gratitude she owed Jerry; she also understood it was imperative that she keep him in her circle of intimates, given what he knew about her. In the immediate post-Liberation period, she followed the U.S. Army as it headed east. The woman who had just a few weeks earlier penned one final slogan for the propaganda service ("Liberators! Liberation! What Liberation?") was now protected by her job on the winning side. Lucie had no problem with such a contradiction if it meant saving her skin and avoiding the shame and infamy of being paraded half naked through the city, head shaved, forehead branded with a red-hot iron, smeared with Mercurochrome, broken and humiliated. She preferred not to think about that.

Jerry was offered a new post with the military court in Reims, after the city was liberated by the Americans. There was no time to waste. With her knowledge of English, Lucie found herself a job as an interpreter at the city's hospital, and she moved in with her sister Zizi's parents-in-law. The idea was to head east, but not too far—nowhere near the concentration camps or the mass graves that were beginning to be discovered. Her knowledge of German was of no use to her now. At last, all the English she had acquired in high school, all those long lists of vocabulary she had learned by heart to outdo the Jewish girls with their English nannies were being put to good use.

Lucie worked as an interpreter during trials of American soldiers, whom she called "liberator-assassins." No doubt she considered them invaders (in German, D-Day is sometimes referred to as "the Invasion"). Some of the cases involved American servicemen accused of acts of violence, including rape, during the heady days of the Liberation. If the accused happened to be Black, Lucie's interpreting, as though she were taking revenge on Friedrich's behalf, would be particularly incriminating. The Black man would pay.

Dreaming bigger, Lucie left France at the first opportunity for America, hoping to start anew on the other side of the Atlantic. It was a hugely risky undertaking, to attempt yet again to switch sides. It was with this plan in mind that, in the spring of 1946, she began an affair in France with an American officer, the son of the wealthy Bostonian owner of a kosher slaughterhouse. The officer, whose name was Theodore but who was known to everyone as Ted, was one of Jerry's closest friends. After he was demobilized, he took Lucie back with him to the United States. His family was Jewish, but this was slightly redeemed by the fact that they were originally from Germany. Ted was a little too Weimar Republic for Lucie's taste but, ever the chameleon, she let it go. Her new boyfriend proudly took her on a tour of the family slaughterhouse: thousands of heads of cattle, industrially slaughtered according to the rules of kashrut. The meat was then transported in a refrigerator railroad car to New York. Lucie hid her repulsion at the sight of the huge carcasses of beef hanging by their feet. She tasted kosher meat for the first time and was amazed to discover it tasted no different than nonkosher meat. Now that she had seen where canned corned beef came from, kosher or not, she would never be able to eat it again.

Had she stayed with Ted a little longer, she would have no doubt begun to pick up some Yiddish. Instead, the pretty young widow moved into an apartment in Boston's Beacon

Hill and began working as a seamstress. By the following year she was posing on the front cover of *Life* magazine.

Lucie moved with consummate ease from the Nazi magazine *Signal* to the weekly *Life*. With everything she had learned about propaganda, she understood the significance of posing in Dior's New Look for an American magazine. It was familiar terrain. She had already studied the competition; French *Signal*, which she had helped launch in 1940, was directly inspired by *Life*, founded four years earlier. It featured the same full-page, often full-color photographs, with the same border, and captions in the same font—Lucie had an insider's appreciation of the readability of the small, bold capital letters in Futura that her uncle Gaston had taught her to recognize—and the same style of gripping reportage, from brilliant sporting exploits to tales of adventurers scaling Alpine peaks and reports in real time of the death camps in Europe that were just beginning to appear. She shared the same pioneering spirit as the American magazine, just not its ideology. How totally convinced Americans were that they were on the right side of history. Let them think it.

Life grew to be so successful that it began trying to win over the readers of its competitor *Vogue* with the occasional fashion spread. Studio fashion photography was a brand-new art form, and haute couture was quintessentially French. Lucie, slim and good-looking, was the perfect model to represent French style. It was only a matter of time before she appeared on the cover.

She also appeared in *Vogue*, *Life*'s frivolous, snobby rival. Lucie may have been a chameleon, but she had her pride: not only did she have no interest in socializing with the glitterati, but so many of the advertisers were Jewish. *Life* put her on the cover, *Vogue* on its inside pages.

However, she soon realized that being on the cover of *Life* was extraordinarily risky and put her in real danger. In France, she had always kept to the shadows, but now she was exposed. *Life* was publishing some of the most gripping photo-reportage of the liberation of the death camps (*what a waste of Margaret Bourke-White's talent to have taken those snaps at Buchenwald!*) as well as detailed reporting direct from the Nuremberg trials. In October 1946, Lucie was horrified to see chilling images of the execution of condemned Nazis.

Ted, her suitor, was keen to get married, but his parents were opposed to what they considered an unorthodox union with an unsuitable young woman. They were apparently prepared to do whatever was required to prevent the marriage from taking place, even going so far as investigating the young woman's background back in Europe. Nothing could have been worse than the prospect of Lucie being unmasked so far from home, living among the enemy. Was it she who left Ted, for fear of being found out, or Ted who couldn't bring himself in the end to put his inheritance on the line? Whatever the reason, Lucie returned to Paris at the end of 1947, alone but with a whitewashed, almost virginal reputation.

During the long journey by ocean liner back to Europe, Lucie, leaning against the ship's rail and gazing out to sea, decided she would stop bleaching her hair. Being blond made her a little too distinctive, and she had her future to think of.

She had come a long way, this olive-skinned granddaughter of Burgundy farmers who had grown up with straw in her clogs, fingers that became cracked and numb when the temperature dropped, treated for head lice with petroleum, locked in the pitch-black cellar as punishment. As a child, she had been cast off like a penniless orphan. Ostensibly, her father, a career soldier, had left the army and was trying to find work. A more plausible reason was that a man so tight-fisted that he switched the electricity meter off at night was happy to save the cost of bringing up his elder daughter by sending her to live with her grandparents.

As long as she lived, Lucie would never have enough time to settle all her scores. That was another reason she remained attached to the gynaeceum. They knew what she had been through. They were there for her.

As a souvenir of her time in America, Lucie always wore a striking gold bracelet of coiled, sculpted links that had either been a breakup offering from Ted, or a parting gift from his relieved parents. She also held on to some of her American ways: she had brought back with her an ice-cream maker, made us mashed potatoes for dinner, and loved the ritual she called "bop and bebop" of pulling the wishbone saved from the chicken carcass. *I won. You lost.*

Jerry, meanwhile, settled in Paris. He and Ted had fallen out over Lucie. Now that was over, he began to dream of being with her again.

Lucie, guided by a sense of priorities and a strong survival instinct, had heard rumors from Paris that the gynaeceum had reformed. Their meetings, in defiance of cautious good sense, had resumed, and the clan, which had been freewheeling for a year and a half, needed a leader.

The gynaeceum was a helpless witness to the seemingly endless postwar purge. Everywhere they looked, people were being convicted of illegal enrichment, of undermining state security (sometimes they were one and the same), or even, the most serious allegation of all, of actively conspiring with the enemy. The gynaeceum was constantly assailed with tales of national humiliation formulated in unfamiliar words and phrases: "rogatory commission," "treason," "bearing arms against France," "fostering business activities with the enemy," "bring in the accused." Always the same stories. What a circus. It was almost like the criminal Courts of Assizes, all those red robes and white ermine. Ah, thought the clan, but our great cause has found only district judges; and indeed, they had committed no crime. All they had cared about was fashion, music, elegance, going out and having fun. But look how that turned out.

All over Europe the enemy was closing in. Uncle Gaston, who had been sitting it out in Switzerland waiting for better days, travelled back and forth between Geneva and Paris. His wife, who was both naïve and intransigent and, above all, had no sense of humor whatsoever, had sought advice from the APA, the Association of Aryan Property Owners, as to how to avoid being forced to give back the comfortable apartment she swore she had acquired legally. The apartment was on Rue de la Chaise, in the Faubourg Saint-Germain, and thus far no one had come forward to claim it. Having a pied-à-terre on Rue de la Chaise, that was the life. She had been a secretary before the war, and I remember her as incredibly snooty, lecturing her visitors, occasionally making fun of me when I came to visit with my mother for not recognizing the French revolutionary writer Madame Roland, whose portrait hung above the mantelpiece. I used to wonder where the painting came from and how it was that she had come to own it.

The circle of the condemned was getting closer to the clan. Were they going to be outed as fascists too? the women whimpered. It wasn't as if they had ever had even the slightest interest in politics. The first blow was the assassination of Philippe Henriot, secretary of state for information in the Vichy government, at dawn on June 28th, 1944, in his state-owned apartment above the ministry on Rue de Solférino. Shot dead in front of his wife by a group of men from the Maquis Resistance brigade. "The bastards!" Terrorists attacking innocent people. Who would ever have imagined such a great man being assassinated?

Henriot was honored with a state funeral, which filled the gynaeceum with pride and somewhat soothed their indignant feelings. According to newspaper reports, several boulevards all over France would henceforth bear the name of the great man. The first would be in Paris. The clan went to pay their last respects to the deceased. The man who had been known as the "voice of France" and of "family values" had also, in his spare time, indulged in a spot of viticulture, cultivating his ancestral vines in the Champagne region and the Gironde. A true man of the soil.

His voice had taken him far: from state radio announcer to minister of information, not to mention an honorary member of the *Milice*, which he had joined out of admiration for Joseph Darnand, its de facto leader. Not that Henriot would ever have hurt a fly. He collected butterflies!

The clan was growing increasingly edgy with the succession of trials and long lists of the guilty in the newspapers. News of the first journalist to be executed, their friend Georges Suarez, on November 9th, 1944, horrified them. Another journalist acquaintance, Jean Hérold-Paquis, was executed on October 11th, 1945. Indicting journalists, in this case a man who was only thirty-three years old—not even seven years older than Lucie—"*the bastards!*" Next it was the turn of Jean Luchaire, who headed the press guild. No one knew exactly what the press guild was, but he had an impressive address book. A bit of a womanizer, but terribly charming. Assassinated on February 22nd, 1946. *His daughter must be in a terrible way. The bastards.* Jean Mamy, journalist and filmmaker, one of Zizi's former lovers, who had promised her a job. What would become of her now? "*Jean Ma-my!*" Zizi murmured in a daze. She had always been pampered and dependent on men and their money. *Oh, Lu-cie!*

Then there was Mussolini. That was a real scandal. Lucie thought he had been hung from a butcher's hook, but the poor thing did have a bit of a tendency to get things confused. She was probably thinking of the Boston slaughterhouse, or the Prussian officers who had made an attempt on Hitler's life on July 20th, 1944, and were shot or hanged in Berlin. Il Duce's corpse was displayed like meat; he was hung by his ankles from the railings of a gas station like an upside-down crucifixion, arms dangling, his mistress alongside him. Assassinated on April 28th, 1945, then paraded for the mob to spit at and disfigure. Lucie was utterly sickened.

The gynaeceum tried to bolster their spirits, seeking information about various friends who had absconded to monasteries in the Italian Alps, like Marcel Déat, founder of the *Rassemblement national-populaire*, a fascist and collaborationist political party. Poor Marcel. They were terribly fond of him. He was from Burgundy too.

Some of their friends had managed to get across the border, but others had been arrested in the mountains of the Tyrol or Bavaria—no one knew exactly where. Geography had never been the women's strong point.

Then there was that poor actress, Mireille Balin, who would never recover from what those bastards did to her. The clan knew her. She might have been one of them. Of Italian descent, she had worked as a fitting room model and a seamstress. An affair with a German officer. Evenings at the embassy. Connections. And then, what they had done to her, eleven of them, in front of her lover.

Fortunately, Franco's Spain was welcoming. Abel Bonnard, a former minister for education, organized tennis tournaments in Madrid with other exiled Frenchmen. Good old Abel. My great-uncle Raphaël used to talk about "Abel and Abetz." It was amazing where public education could get you.

Lucie returned to Paris in 1948 to find the clan reunited, laundered, so to speak, in the great whitewashing that followed the Liberation. The uncles had settled into their new lives, their reputations whiter than white. The family's honor was intact.

The eldest of the uncles, Gaston, the important journalist, spent most of his time in Geneva.

The middle uncle, the pharmacist, remained in Vichy, behind the counter of his dispensary, where he was unlikely to be bothered.

The youngest uncle, diminutive and blue-eyed, retired to a pretty village on the English Channel. With his soft voice and rolling r's he made everyone forget his past as editor-in-chief of a glossy magazine devoted to movie stars and film news, in a collaborationist version proudly based in the same building as the propaganda service.

Under the guise of an innocent gossip publication, it was in fact an organ for promoting the films of Continental, the influential Nazi-controlled production company, established in France in 1940 as a subsidiary of the German UFA, the *Universal Film Aktiengesellschaft*. Its frothy articles lulled its mostly female readers into accepting French films produced by the occupying forces. Not politics, but entertainment!

This uncle had always very much enjoyed his job; it allowed him plenty of mistresses, and he had even sold the family home in Burgundy, where Lucie was born, after he inherited it in 1943, in order to buy himself a beautiful car. His latest conquest was, according to whispers among the clan, a Jewish woman.

My mother used to take me to visit him when I was a child. She persuaded him to let me leaf through piles of faded copies of the magazine. Stars of the French silver screen photographed in three-quarter view, their chins tilted upward and their eyebrows heavily plucked, frozen in time, still awaiting their moment of glory.

Lucie felt an emptiness she needed to fill. She wanted to settle down. She swore to herself she would have a child before she turned thirty. She had always dreamed of having a child with Friedrich, who was so focused on the ovulation and follicle issues of his mice but refused to let her become a mother. She was twenty-nine now; she still had a year to go. She was very pretty, and her many friends and acquaintances introduced her to potential suitors. Among them was a handsome man called Charles, whom a number of her girlfriends had their eye on. He must have seemed rather cautious compared to the radical young Nazi cavalrymen she had known, but by the same token there was something reassuring about him. Lucie could imagine making a future with him, not least because marrying him meant she could change her name, which would be useful, and climb the social ladder, which suited her ambitions; in short, she could rebuild her life.

Charles was the scion of a well-to-do family of landowners, with notarial deeds going back generations. There were local grandees, pharmacists, and doctors among them too. His mother had been an only child, and her mother as well. This appealed to Lucie, not least because it indicated a concentration of capital. A seventeenth-century mansion with a courtyard and garden in a provincial town in inland France. Protestants forced to convert to Catholicism by the *dragonnades*, the king's dragoons. Jansenism. A Bach cantata every day. An obsession with social and ethnic endogamy.

Charles was a brilliant graduate of the newly established school for training senior civil servants. Tall, blond, and blue-eyed, he looked a little like Friedrich, and marriage to him would, in a way, offer a means for Lucie to bear Friedrich's children.

As a teenager, I was fascinated with the story of Susanne Albrecht, a young German woman with a sullen expression, daughter of a Hamburg lawyer, who joined the Red Army Faction. In 1977, she facilitated the murder of her sister's godfather, the wealthy banker Jürgen Ponto, whom she called Uncle Jürgen. With two fellow RAF members, she went to his house with a bunch of flowers, and he opened the front door to her, suspecting nothing. After the murder, Albrecht fled to East Germany, where she rebuilt her life on the other side of the Iron Curtain. She took a new name, Ingrid Jäger, and lived under the protection of the Stasi, the state secret police. For thirteen years, Susanne of the Baader-Meinhof Gang lived a quiet life as a translator in East Berlin. She married a physicist named Becker, who knew nothing of her past, and had a son. When the Berlin Wall came down, Ingrid Becker confessed her past to her husband. In the suburbs of East Berlin, she and her husband sat and waited for the police to come and arrest her.

It was not until much later that I recognized certain parallels between Albrecht's life and that of my mother, who, with her two successive marriages, had twice changed her surname and may have adopted pseudonyms at various points. On her return from exile in the United States, she had once again begun a new life. Back in the city of her past deeds, bearing the name and social status of her second husband, she transformed herself into a staunchly bourgeois housewife. She became an invisible Parisian in a city where it is entirely possible to live a clandestine life in full view of the world. Her new husband was ignorant of her past—or perhaps he just didn't want to know.

I remember, in the 1960s, watching my mother on the television news baptizing an oil tanker, smashing a bottle of champagne against its immense hull with her Mona Lisa smile. I think of my mother at home in Paris, about to go out for the evening with my father, in a pair of long dark-purple leather gloves that reached up to her elbows. My mother, the consummate hostess, welcoming her husband's guests. She was impossible to pin down.

Lucie soon tired of domestic and married life. Real life was elsewhere. Charles may have borne a passing resemblance to Friedrich, but he was not Friedrich. Though they occasionally went away on vacation together, leaving their daily life behind, their marriage was more of a strategic alliance than a love match: Lucie liberated Charles from his staid family background, while Charles offered her security. But having lived with such intensity, she was now discovering how very dull everyday life could be.

When they first visited Les Chomettes together, the locals confused Charles with Friedrich. It was as if Friedrich had been reincarnated, which made Lucie very happy. But Charles bore all the prejudices of his class: he did not like the poor, and he had this awkward habit of always trying to come across as working-class. The locals may not have had much material wealth, but they were no fools. Charles would adopt a local accent with people who meant nothing to him, but whom his conventional Catholic upbringing obliged him to acknowledge.

Worse, with the birth of each successive child, Charles found he didn't enjoy fatherhood, and Lucie discovered she was not made to be a mother. What a terrible disillusionment. But she had set her own trap. She refused to breast-feed, for fear it would ruin her breasts. After each child was born, she bandaged her breasts tightly to prevent the milk coming in and maintain her figure. The children took up all her time and alienated her from other adults. She often entrusted us to others to care for, in the countryside, in town, to relatives or domestics. Sometimes we thrived, sometimes not. We were handed over to an erotomaniac former prostitute, a dodgy couple who resembled Victor Hugo's unscrupulous swindlers the Thénardiers in *Les Misérables,* a psychotic creature who was full of goodwill but severely damaged.

"Come along," she instructed her unnerved offspring.

"*Lebensborn* children never made such a fuss." In her view, the only thing that mattered was that children got enough fresh air. The way she dropped it into the conversation, she clearly saw nothing amiss about the Nazis' Lebensborn program, where women considered to be racially pure were encouraged to give birth in specially established homes.

Lucie left me in the care of Eugénie, my dedicated nanny, in Picardy, north of Paris, as it happens not far from the only Lebensborn home to have been established in France. Eugénie had brought up another foster child who, coincidentally, shared a first name with Pétain. She told me his father had been a "nasi." She was probably being a little strict when she tied little Fifi to the radiator. He committed suicide as an adult.

Eugénie looked terribly slovenly and down-at-heel. She always wore a blue floral nylon apron-dress, slippers, and wire-rimmed state-issued spectacles through which she peered with blinking eyes. She used two combs to hold back her white shoulder-length hair that was flat at the top and frizzy at the ends like a grown-out perm. She adored vermicelli soup, which I later learned was a dish served daily in the SS. It was a horrible shock when she took her masticator out of her pocket: a pair of meat shears for shredding the meat on her plate that she didn't have the teeth for. I was always relieved when the device was returned to its cage in her apron pocket.

Eugénie was part of a community of wartime collaborators. She was the girlfriend of a former member of the *Milice* who had been the managing director of the antisemitic journal *Je suis partout*, and the press attaché for *Milice* founder Joseph Darnand. In 1944 her lover was sentenced to life imprisonment with forced labor and sent to Clairvaux Prison. After he was pardoned, he went back to live with his wife and little boy, who was born in 1943, but he still paid the odd visit to his old mistress. There was a quarter of a century between them.

Their relationship was stormy. The woman I called Mamie Génia intoned her lover's surname almost as though it were a curse. She never called him by his first name. Once, in a fury, she ripped up a photograph of the two of them lying on the grass and smiling up at the camera. She told me that he had been in the "malice" and had worked with an "important monsieur," but now he had no work. He stole into the house like a thief; Eugénie gave him a bit of money, they fought, and the thief departed.

Eugénie was odd, but Lucie let it go. The important thing was that her children lived in a world that was coherent.

Many years later I got a job in publishing, only to discover that the son of the *milicien* of my childhood was now director of the publishing house where I worked and was also married to my second cousin, the granddaughter of the uncle who was once editor-in-chief of the collaborationist film magazine. They are no longer together, but sometimes I spot from afar one or the other of their children in the foyer of the apartment building where their father still lives on the top floor. Respecting the family interdiction, I never introduce myself. I did, though, go to the wedding of their daughter. She was stunning, with her little nose and wide, sky-blue eyes—the family eyes. She wore a wedding dress frothing with tulle and was surrounded by so many young people it was impossible to work out which was her husband.

Lucie was happy; the world was coherent.

All the same, there was something disturbing about my nanny. Sometimes I had the impression there were multiple Eugénies in her head. She had five cats, including a Snowy and a Blacky. They let me stroke them. They were allowed to do whatever they wanted, though she always yelled when they climbed on the furniture and lapped water from the jug. Sometimes, in a fit of anger, she threw them into the cellar and asphyxiated them with gas she got from the pharmacist. They disappeared. The house was quiet. Then more arrived. She gave them the same names: Snowy, Blacky... One day this lot disappeared too. And so it went on.

Lucie sighed and paid the nanny. She didn't have a choice. That must be the very definition of Darwinism.

Apparently Eugénie had inherited her houses in the Oise from her father, who had been a dockworker at Saint-Ouen. He had a business card that read "locksmith-mechanic-factory installation." That was all that was said about him, which was perhaps for the best, given that it was unusual for a dockworker to make a fortune in real estate—except in Saint-Ouen, where the warehouses had been used by the Germans to store stolen goods. It was small-fry, nothing fancy—but even miniature livestock makes manure.

Eugénie seemed to have no idea how to manage her money. The checks she wrote during the occasional romantic getaway with her *milicien* always bounced and, after an apologetic but insistent statement by the judges—not the first—she was duly fined. She began selling off her houses, including to my great-uncle Raphaël, who, with his easy manner and Parisian drawl, she addressed familiarly as Rafi.

Driving her 2CV back to Paris through the gloomy forests of the Oise, Lucie imagined the dialogue at her trial:

"Have you ever been a Nazi?"

"Of course! I was a very happy Nazi."

"You really were a Nazi?"

"Why not?"

"Do you know, you are the very first person we have ever heard confess to it."

Lucie imagined the entire courtroom staring at her and burst out laughing. Saved from prison on grounds of honesty and loyalty.

Sometimes my mother would be overwhelmed with sadness after saying goodbye to her little girl. Unable to see through her tears, she would pull over onto a grassy stretch along the road, switch off the engine, and cry her eyes out. Everything was mixed up in her head. It was so difficult being a mother. So hard to keep going on her own. After a while she pulled herself together, delved into her purse for a handkerchief, then rifled around in the glove compartment, finding the piece of chamois leather that had come in handy during the war to filter fuel from German planes, eventually laying hands on a cloth handkerchief, which she used to dab the tear stains off her face in the rearview mirror. Then, chin down, hairpins clamped between her lips, she looped a headscarf around her chignon, knotted it at the nape of her neck, scraped a little lipstick onto her lips from the very bottom of the tube—the treasures in the little car's glove compartment were apparently inexhaustible—and grimaced into the rearview mirror to make sure there was none on her teeth. Finally, she dabbed some more lipstick onto her cheekbones and checked her face in the mirror one last time. She was ready to go. She pulled out the choke, then listened to the engine resist for a moment until it started with a cough. She maneuvered the car off the roadside and back onto the pavement. It was the same Citroën 2CV—the French version of the Volkswagen Beetle, the "people's car" commissioned by the Führer in 1938—she had been driving since the early 1950s. To Lucie, it was a mythical object, the receptacle of all her brooding aspirations. A lifetime vehicle: the only car she ever drove. It was nicknamed in France the walnut shell, the nuns' car, *deudeuche*. No other car would have suited her. She paid so little attention to the rules of the road that it was only the sluggishness of the engine that kept her safe.

As night began to fall, she switched on the headlights. It was what Friedrich used to call "the witching hour." She leaned over the steering wheel and scanned the road. It reminded her of the blackout. Soon it would be pitch-black, the road ahead lit only by the car's pale-yellow headlights. She resumed her monologue, locked in her memories, on the verge of madness.

It was not as if she lacked support. There was her family, the inner circle, the gynaeceum, who clung to her like mollusks to a rock. They constituted the framework of her life—though they sometimes felt like a millstone around her neck. They had the merit of being there, like pieces of furniture, part of the décor, protectors of memory. They had gone through the same experiences, shared that world with her, part of the happy few who had known it. She was the queen bee, and her hive was more or less under control. They knew one another so well.

There were her former in-laws, Friedrich's family, that of her first, eternal, true husband. Lucie remained in contact with Friedrich's sister throughout their lives, her faithful ally, with her proudly assumed and unwavering Nazi convictions. When she was twenty-nine, clad in a dark suit rather like those worn during the Occupation by the women known as the *souris grises*—gray-suited young French women who worked as secretaries for the German occupying army—she married a pale man, a little head-in-the-clouds, so lackluster it was almost as if he had already ascended to heaven. This was in 1950, six years after Friedrich's death, and his stern-featured sister still carried herself as if she were her brother's widow. She continued to carry the torch, the true Nazi of the family, increasingly indifferent to everything else.

It was not so long ago that mothers were giving their sons to the Führer, but all the same, Lucie was a little shaken by how hard her sister-in-law had become.

Then there were Lucie's other in-laws, from her marriage to Charles. They simply generated unplumbed levels of boredom. Apart from her cousins' children, who had not—or not yet—become bourgeois, petty, and noxious, being with them was an endless round of empty chatter and tedious anecdotes sprung from narrow provincial minds. Her authoritarian mother-in-law, whom Lucie always addressed as Madame, was unsettled by this daughter-in-law who refused to bow to convention. Brisk, efficient, bordering on rude, Lucie found it hard to disguise her impatience at the disordered way of thinking wrought by Catholic bigotry. Even their antisemitism was pathetic. No genuine ideology. At least Lucie's antisemitism was bold. Her manners horrified her husband's family, though they politely put it down to eccentricity. *Oh, Lu-cie...*

From time to time, as the years went by, Lucie looked back on her life. She had worn so many masks that had both helped and hindered her, methodically erasing past lives when they no longer suited her current reality. But for decades now, her life had followed a straight and narrow path, and she permitted herself the occasional affair simply to make life more bearable.

As for the horrors of the last war, well, *they must have done something to deserve it, no*? She hated the ghastly expression "war profiteers." Everyone knew that the apartment on the Place des Pyramides had been vacant when she and Friedrich moved in, but it had been the tenant's choice to move out, and he had had the means. How was that Lucie's fault? The couple had been looking for a place to settle down. It wasn't as if she had posted a classified advertisement: "Couple looking to purloin an apartment." And when you think how hard she had worked! She deserved a suitable recompense. Their apartment on Place des Pyramides—aptly named—and the one on Quai de l'Archevêché—an address too religious for their secular family—allocated to her sister's husband, were both in acknowledgement of services rendered.

Lucie was never very interested in what she called "things." "They're just *things*," she would say, referring to confiscated property, a term she employed frequently. To justify herself, she bandied about a legal term, "in trust," which meant "assigned to a person in good faith." Lucie was very fond of the notion of good faith. Someone gives something to someone else, for them to give to someone else. The real owner is the "community of the people." This was not yet law in France, but it would be. She also liked to quote the Latin adage *Uti possidetis juris*, which she thought meant something like "You possess what is already in your possession." As far as Lucie was concerned, it was always a question of possession.

With extraordinary resourcefulness, she gave to one person, took from another, returned, exchanged, sold, bought back, reallocated, and disposed as she pleased of "things," her own as well as those of others. Whenever she arrived somewhere new, she would always look around to see what she could leave with or negotiate for. It could just as well have been an article of clothing as an apartment. She always renamed her newly acquired possessions, supposing it might have otherwise been possible to trace them back to their original owners.

No, she had no regrets. On the contrary. If all the French had been on the right side, Germany would have won the war. You only had to look at what a prosperous country Germany had become once more. Friedrich was no longer there, but he would be back. They had to remain unchanged for each another. They had done everything right. This was just a difficult period they had to get through. The Reich would be reborn, in one form or another. Vichy would continue. It was just a dirty trick that history had played on them. Fortunately, there were plenty of people who remained unbowed and unbeaten. As Friedrich, with his habitual touch of pomposity, had once written to Lucie: "We shall stride toward the future, our consciences clear and our heads held high, faithful to our conception of the world and of this life." Now it was Lucie's turn to address Friedrich. *My honor is my fidelity. Vae victis*, woe to the vanquished. History is always written by the victors. And to the victor go the spoils.

"Things" were always perfectly straightforward. It was people who complicated them.

4

Though carefully kept at arm's length by my mother, my great-uncle Raphaël constantly and somewhat paradoxically hovered against the backdrop of our family life, arousing both disapproval and envy. He was frequently talked about but, ever the outcast, never invited to any gathering, large or small, formal or informal. As a teenager, if I wanted to see him, I had to traipse all the way over to his apartment in the exiled territories of northern Paris, where people like us never set foot.

Only once, after he was decorated, did my mother agree to accompany me, with a mixture of pride, embarrassment, and a touch of contempt, as if this trifling honor might somehow reflect back on her or her family. For it turned out that Raphaël was famous. I remember my astonishment when I heard his familiar voice on the car radio one morning. It seemed that he was held in high esteem by the entire world, and when he died, in his nineties, all the newspapers carried a full-page obituary.

Yet always this silence from my mother. Why was Raphaël ostracized by the rest of the family? He endured his banishment stoically and could always be reached by telephone.

One evening, after a performance at the Royal Opera House in Versailles, where he had been toasted by *le Tout Paris*, he said to me, full of pent-up rage, "Tell your parents that I am a *someone*."

He must once have been very handsome and, despite a little thickening around the waist, he still cut a fine figure as he surveyed the world through his piercing pale blue eyes. Tall, glamorous, flamboyant, imposing, and amusing, he was also venomous and power-hungry. In front of an audience of socialites he barely knew, he was capable of sacrificing a friend's trust for a witty remark. He was never quite the same with different people; he was always "doing a Raphaël." He was famous for his anecdotes, and recounted them well, always carefully setting up the punch line. He was supremely snobbish and loved nothing more than laying into what he called mockingly "distinguishment and refinery." He modified names and numbers as it suited him, omitting, embellishing, or knitting together two different stories. Not everyone always believed him, even though he sometimes told the truth. Everyone was convinced of their own version of Raphaël.

His upbringing had been very traditional. "As a child," he once told me, "my parents scared me; as an adult, I intimidated them. We never really knew each other." He added, "I always knew I liked boys." That was the main reason Lucie, with her fascist ideals and aversions, disliked him. She abhorred what she called pederasts, especially in her own family.

Harking back to a lonely childhood, Raphaël said he had always preferred playing with Dresden porcelain figurines rather than toy soldiers. He would take a porcelain marquise, a water carrier, and a shepherdess, and act out stories beneath the pergola in the garden. The first time he saw a play performed by a troupe of French actors, that was it: He had found his vocation. The theater would be his home.

His father, whom he hated on account of his thick neck and lack of sophistication, married twice. His first wife, Marie-Thérèse, my great-grandmother, was nicknamed the barefoot countess, though in fact she was not a countess at all but a farmer's daughter. My mother always called her Grand-mère Abramo. She died young, leaving her widower to bring up their daughter, Hermine, my grandmother.

The second time was an arranged marriage, with a solid prenuptial agreement keeping the bride's and groom's assets separate. My great-grandfather's new wife was a little past her prime, but heir to a wealthy landowning family. Miraculously, she bore a son, Raphaël, nine years younger than his half-sister, Hermine, who mothered the little boy and was always sensitive to his "difference."

Years later, Raphaël still telephoned his cash-strapped half-sister every day to offer his support—moral, not financial—after her marriage to my grandfather, a most unsuitable man.

With the demise of Raphaël's parents, money allied with money. Raphaël, grandson through his mother of wealth, was now rich, while Herminette, the granddaughter of a farmer, was stuck in semipoverty. He became a landowner; she remained a tenant. All her life, my mother, Lucie, Herminette's daughter, harbored a deep, if unavowed resentment about this. It seemed so unfair that Raphaël, who had no children of his own, should be rich and not her. He didn't even give any of his fortune to his beloved sister's children. He did, however, favor one of them, Zizi, inviting her to accompany him to grand social occasions while snubbing her sister, Lucie, the unsophisticated little country bumpkin.

He'd pay for it one day, of that Lucie was absolutely determined.

Aged sixteen, Raphaël left his life in the provinces for the Paris of the Roaring Twenties. The handsome young libertine made his entry into this sophisticated world by selling his body to a series of aristocratic lovers, some of whom were very married and even had children; these were men who understood about discreet envelopes and beautiful gifts. Raphaël began with a few pieces of jewelry, over time receiving more pieces of increasing value, until his collection rivaled that of a Roman emperor or a Renaissance prince.

I remember nuggets of solid gold, huge amethyst crosses, cameos on long chains, signet rings, and several stylish pairs of cuff links. He bowed down to us in the oriental style, as if burdened by the weight of these scandalous rewards, without vulgarity, but with pure satisfaction, holding out to visitors a beautiful, manicured hand that seemed to hint at all the caressing it had done.

Raphaël the provocateur—always ready to twist one bon mot into another—liked to drawl, enunciating each syllable, "I slept with whomever I needed to." He did indeed sleep around a great deal, even indiscriminately, especially if there was an opportunity for eliciting favors. He picked men up easily and rarely got attached.

With his talent for self-deprecating humor, one of his earliest acquisitions was a "whore's bed," a chaise longue that had supposedly belonged to the great tragic actress Rachel (it turned out to be a fake, but he didn't really care: what mattered was the opportunity for an anecdote about the chance encounter between larger History and personal history).

For well over a decade, Raphaël led an easy life of pleasure, peppered with a succession of favors and gifts until, in his early thirties, he met the love of his life, who was to become his lifelong companion and mentor. His lover was heir to a large rubber fortune. A chemist like his father, he realized that synthetic rubber was the future. He was now living in France, where the family's factory was located, and consolidating his fortune by supplying the Germans, who needed rubber for the war effort.

The two men shared a love of music. They were both great aesthetes, and together they traveled the length and breadth of Europe. This passion-filled grand tour was their honeymoon.

Raphaël led the life of a dilettante; as he liked to say, he "took his pleasures seriously." Guided by his lover, he read the classics, studied musical theory, practiced the piano, and discovered that he had perfect pitch, a talent he perhaps should have cultivated. He also turned out to have hyperacusis: he could hear things most people could not.

With their love of music and obsession with beauty, the couple took their talents off to Venice, where they strutted about like peacocks in a palazzo on the Grand Canal, listening complacently to the echo of Mussolini's boots, which hardly disturbed their pleasure. "Venice is not a city, it is a stage," Raphaël liked to say.

Once he invited the teenage Lucie to spend a few weeks in the Venetian palazzo. She returned home stunned by the splendor. It was also her first encounter with fascism. Was it really possible to live like that? But back in Paris, she found herself once again treated like an impoverished relative who had briefly crawled out of her burrow.

The Caesar-like demeanor of Il Duce rather appealed to Raphaël, who was not insensitive to the revolutionary eroticism of the handsome young Italian soldiers in uniform, preparing to whip Italy into shape. He and his lover invited everyone to their home and were received all over the city. It seemed as if Italians never threw a party without enlivening it with a concert. Raphaël the dilettante occasionally doubted he was truly a "someone," despite his lover's support.

A photograph taken at the time shows him in a white tuxedo, leaning nonchalantly against a Venetian well. He is smiling. He is loved. The fascist years were his time of glory.

Back in Paris in 1939, just before the outbreak of war, Raphaël became a well-known figure in artistic and social circles. There was one particular viscountess, a charming woman, whom he counted as a friend, having met her in Rome before the war and then back in Paris. A true European. She and her husband were "one of us." She entertained *le Tout Paris*—everyone who was anyone in occupied Paris, *bien sûr*. Raphaël summed it up with a pithy phrase: "We knew how to have fun."

Once again, my mother, Lucie, slipped back into the shadows. She had examinations to prepare for and needed to figure out how to obtain a scholarship so she could continue her studies. She worked hard and bided her time.

Raphaël moved seamlessly from fascist Italy to the so-called phony war in France with barely a change of scenery. When he was called up, he managed, through some mysterious channel, to get a job in the army's film department, where his duties consisted of watching French and German newsreels. In June 1940 he escaped Paris like almost everyone else, swapping his Salmson coupé for a small pickup truck provided by the army. He left his jewelry and his beautiful car behind for his great-nieces to look after.

Later he said that he would rather have stayed behind to enjoy the beautiful National Socialist bodies with muscles "like chocolate bars" marching into Paris in serried ranks. When he did eventually come back he discreetly took a steady companion—usefully, a German—whom he met walking along the Grands Boulevards; he must have rather liked him, because he kept a photograph of him on display long after their affair was over. Apparently the man ended up getting shot. He painted several Expressionist-style portraits of Raphaël.

The Nazi lover worked for the *Dienststelle Westen*, the Western Agency, the Nazi service responsible for the systematic seizure of possessions from apartments expropriated from Jews. What a marvelous time it was! Raphaël was invited to help himself from a large warehouse somewhere around the Bastille neighborhood (he was always a touch evasive when it came to questions of location). He could take whatever he wanted.

If you are going to help yourself, you may as well take the nice stuff.

His tastes were both eclectic and discerning. He never alluded to the Jews who had suffered to his advantage. "To each his own . . . bad taste," he declared with a wry smile, perhaps unaware that this bon mot was his own version of the now controversial German expression *Jedem das Seine*—to each his own—that was displayed over the entrance of the Buchenwald concentration camp.

Some of his finest pieces had come at a bargain price from a well-known antique store that he always called, mystifyingly, Rue de Téhéran, near the Faubourg Saint-Honoré, run by an old flame. Raphaël presented it as though he had done the dealer a favor; but when the man came back from the camps after the war, he demanded the return of his property.

I had never heard of Rue de Téhéran other than in their coded language, and I had no idea at the time what this metonymy signified.

Anyhow, deals flourished.

At least Raphaël did not embroider the details of these items of furniture with extravagant designations of style or period, as did his nieces, my mother and aunt, hoping thus to erase their provenance. Most of the time, he simply said he knew nothing at all about them. He claimed to find them aesthetically beautiful, that was all, as if they had a life of their own, and had never belonged to anyone.

One day, sitting on the bus, Raphaël overheard some fellow passengers gossiping about an apartment on Boulevard Saint-Martin. It just so happened to be where he and his lover lived. There were parties, private concerts, a group of transvestites who held orgies, despite the curfew! *Someone really ought to inform the police.*

Raphaël's blood ran cold. He realized they were talking about him and his lover. They were going to need to be more discreet. He decided to formalize the spontaneous concerts they had been holding; under the direction of his lover, he took over a musical ensemble that needed a manager, appointing himself its impresario. As manager of the ensemble, he was entitled to a percentage of the artists' fees and profits. And so he began to put on concerts for the public.

Raphaël was always discreet about precisely how he had brought about the revival of the ensemble, but one day, watching a German newsreel from the Occupation, I caught a glimpse of him from behind at a Mozart concert in the Tuileries Garden.

He was kept so occupied during the Occupation that the prospect of it coming to an end was beginning to worry him;

when, in the spring of 1944, he was invited to produce a major musical event, he realized he would be better off getting out of Paris. He and his lover set their sights on the south of France. They moved into a small, remote farmhouse, where they kept themselves to themselves.

In June 1945 he returned to the capital, reputation intact, to take up the post of vice president of the *Comité d'épuration des gens du spectacle*, the entertainment industry's purge commission, which met at the all-too-familiar former premises of the propaganda service on the Champs-Élysées. He had been co-opted onto the committee by its president, an orchestra conductor who had been active in the Resistance but had also voiced the French version of the notorious antisemitic 1940 movie *Jud Süss*. The two men were, officially, relatively uncompromised. Several of Raphaël's old acquaintances from the artistic world appeared before the court, and he settled a number of cases in ways that augured well for his future.

Not only had the purger managed to spare himself from being purged, but he was also whitewashing the reputations of his peers. He had managed to join the victorious side, just like his niece Lucie. The chameleon effect is a constant in my family.

Finding the postwar atmosphere in Paris stultifying, Raphaël soon went back to the south of France, where, with the backing of a generous female patron, he helped found a classical music festival that was to become one of Europe's great operatic events, modeled on the Salzburg Festival—not that he ever made the slightest allusion to Salzburg. He went on to serve as the festival's artistic director for several years, during which he introduced the French to open-air performances in outdoor theaters, what is known in German as *Freilichtspiele*, which he had first encountered on his prewar travels through Europe. He built his reputation on Mozart, and he seemed to be in such an intimate relationship with *Così fan tutte*, *The Magic Flute*, *Idomeneo*, *The Marriage of Figaro*, *Don Giovanni*, and *The Abduction from the Seraglio* that when he spoke about them it was as if they were people, not operas. The countess in *Figaro* seemed to him more real and charming than any real-life countess. It was as though he were still staging scenes for imaginary princesses under the pergola in his childhood garden. He was entirely unbothered by the horrific stories that were coming out about the war. He preferred those involving powdered wigs, in the style of Marie-Antoinette, in what were to become his festival standards.

Slowly but surely, Raphaël's standing and reputation had changed. Many German artists—some of whom, as former Nazis, were no longer able to perform in their native country—conveniently remembered Raphaël, or he them, in addition to various compatriots with compromising pasts (and thus compromised futures) who came to work for him.

Refusing to go into any detail, Raphaël simply drawled, "They had a few problems after the war. Couldn't find any work." Where necessary, he provided them with a sort of denazification certificate, what the Germans mockingly nicknamed a *Persilschein*, an allusion to Persil washing powder that "washes whiter than white." Armed with this free pass, the great launderer simultaneously laundered his own reputation. It was becoming a bit of a habit in the family.

Conductors, composers, musicians, singers, painters, and stage designers were deep in Raphaël's debt for the new lease on life he offered them. He founded a sort of troupe that allowed the outcasts to blend in with the crowds beneath the Provençal sun. He certainly had flair. Mozart, ideal for the situation, was performed more than any other composer: untouchable, since he had died young, centuries ago, and unarguable, being both famous and little-performed in France. Above suspicion. Mozart erased everything. He was the ultimate reputational launderer to whom no one could object. The Archangel Raphaël kept watch over everyone.

When his companion died, relatively young, after twenty-five years together, Raphaël lost not only his great love but his mentor, protector, and strength. For the last four decades of his life, he kept a photograph of his lover, taken at the famous Harcourt photography studio, beside his bed, a branch of dried boxwood wedged into the frame. His lover, solemn and powerful, gazed out at him through his tortoiseshell spectacles, powerless now to guide and protect him. From then on it was Raphaël's turn to fall prey to younger men, always provisional, occasionally kind, often on the make. Never again was he to encounter a true kindred spirit.

All through his life Raphaël somehow managed to extricate himself from every awkward situation. He had this way of blatantly flouting taboos that concealed something darker; his motto was "The truth, you know, is so much simpler."

But his vindictive niece Lucie, my mother, was biding her time. She would not be passed over so easily. As soon as her uncle had lost his lover, Lucie—Machiavellian, cunning, and not in the slightest taken in by all this talk of Mozart—began blackmailing him, and continued to do so for the rest of his life.

Lucie claimed to have a compromising letter in her possession concerning a denunciation that my great-uncle had sent in 1943 to the Commissariat-General for Jewish Affairs. It is possible that this letter did not really exist, but Raphaël had written others, so it might as well have.

I remember the relentless threat that the letter would be divulged. My mother always swore she had it in her possession and managed to make Raphaël believe her. She went into more and more detail over the years, but never showed it to him. She described the pale blue vellum, the letterhead, the irregular spelling in black ink. It was all quite plausible. My great-uncle, who although he knew the entire works of Molière by heart, was quite capable of asking, with a baffled look on his face, "Is it *tomorrow* with one *m* or two?"

The contents of the letter were equally credible. Raphaël and his lover had lived like lords during the Occupation. Meat was served at their generous table twice a day, and every guest received a packet of cigarettes as a parting gift.

According to my mother, Raphaël had written to Louis Darquier de Pellepoix, the Vichy government's commissioner for Jewish affairs, to lodge a complaint about a certain Monsieur d'Eschelette, a provisional administrator of "Jewish property," appointed by the Commissariat-General.

The administrator may have been provisional, but the administration was definitive, and it was the job of the PA, as he was known, who was paid in a percentage of the receipts, to off-load the property in his hands as swiftly as possible.

The existence of this denunciation letter could not have emerged at a worse time for Raphaël. When had he written it? He wasn't sure about anything. It was his lover, not long deceased, who had dealt with practical matters. Raphaël was beginning to make a name for himself in Paris and had recently been appointed artistic adviser at the Opéra Garnier.

Of course, he relished telling the story of how during the Occupation he had once been summoned to the Gestapo headquarters on Rue des Saussaies and questioned for several hours before being released. One thing did not preclude the other, however, and if this letter were ever to be revealed—if it indeed existed—it would come to light that in 1943 Raphaël had demanded the dismissal of this Monsieur d'Eschelette, for dealing with the dozen or so Jewish businesses in his charge with culpable tardiness.

Raphaël had apparently urged the provisional administrator to do his duty as a patriot, in the very street where he lived, in response to which Monsieur d'Eschelette is said to have replied that he had sent the Jewess, as he called her—my mother pretended to be reading the letter over the telephone, waving her hands around as she spoke—who owned the apartment buildings a letter of formal notice, to which he had received no reply. If the Commissariat wanted to check for itself and relieve this inadequate liquidator of his duties, Raphaël would be happy to recommend one of his acquaintances, another PA, a proud Frenchman who would accomplish his responsibilities quickly (the word was underlined in the text). This was no time for *patience or sympathy*, it was the time for *resolve*. If this were done, the Aryanization of all remaining inhabited properties in the buildings would pick up pace. The letter ended with Raphaël affirming that he was available to meet at the Commissariat's convenience.

Is it possible that Raphaël was genuinely thinking of the public good? He always talked about Pétain working for the good of France, but never went into detail. It seemed less a question of getting this Monsieur d'Eschelette dismissed than of finding a job for an acquaintance. But in either case, my great-uncle had compromised his position.

There were some other stubborn facts: During the Occupation, Raphaël's lover had acquired several apartments in Paris, situated behind the Butte Montmartre. The buildings, many with boutiques on the ground floor, had been almost entirely emptied of their inhabitants. Of course, the lover had paid for them—a modest sum, but he had paid all the same.

As far as Raphaël was concerned, there was no way these purchases involved fraud or ill-gotten gains; they were fair remuneration, a sort of commission for bringing in businesses, around 10 or 15 percent, which gives an idea of the number of apartments that fell into the lap of the Commissariat-General for Jewish Affairs—in other words, the French state.

Little by little, Raphaël and his lover became agents, for anyone and everyone. They took commission twice over: real estate went to the French, while furniture and other transportable goods went to the Germans. It was a small world, where the same people did business with one another, and for every deal there was a commission to be paid.

It is probable that my mother never had this letter in her possession. But although she was almost certainly bluffing, her uncle believed her. The Place des Pyramides in Paris, where Friedrich and Lucie had lived during the Occupation, is not far from the Place des Petits-Pères, where the Commissariat-General for Jewish Affairs was based, and Lucie was acquainted with the chief of staff, an old comrade of her father's from the Great War. She claimed to have the letter, and it is possible she had seen it, or that it had been handed over to her. There were so many such letters.

The one thing that is certain is that my mother wanted the apartments for her family, and the timely discovery of this letter of denunciation was key to a scheme that had been brewing for years.

When, after the war, no one returned to claim the apartments, they were rented out. My mother, full of envy and fury, repeatedly pointed out during tense exchanges with her uncle that he had become owner by usucapion, the acquisition of property by prolonged and undisturbed possession—a legal term that, in its homophony, is close enough to *usurpation* to be entirely appropriate.

Raphaël couldn't remember—his lover had always taken care of everything, dictating letters to him for him to sign. Raphaël had never even looked at his own bank statements. He had no interest in such niceties. Had the Commissariat-General for Jewish Affairs sold these assets to Raphaël's lover through the provisional administrator? Or had his lover bought them at auction through the Land Registration Department, or the Aryan Property Owners' Association? Had he paid in cash through an accommodating notary? It was all such a muddle in his head.

Anyway, that was just how things were in that period. It was idiotic, all this talk of collaboration. Everyone had been involved. It was not as if he were to blame for any of it. Honestly, "spoliation," "denunciation," such big words! And how exactly had Lucie managed to get hold of the letter? She refused to say, of course. Had the letters not been burned after all, as Darquier had promised him they would be?

One thing was certain: Raphaël's lover had had the money to pay for the apartments. They were all compromised.

A decade after the war ended, the lover contracted a kidney disease that could not be cured. Raphaël could not inherit from his lifelong companion.

Lucie began scheming. Her father was a manager at a large bank. On behalf of the family, he agreed to issue a certificate stating that the apartments had been purchased by

Raphaël from his lover. Using this document, they were able to formalize the sale. An accommodating notary was found who was prepared to sign it.

For thirty years, Raphaël had lived off the income from these apartments, which financed his lifestyle and that of any number of hangers-on, most of whom who were interested less in his charms than in his money. Raphaël was a willing dupe, believing each new lover to be a kindred spirit, or at least decent-hearted. But con artists of all stripes, sometimes vouched for by duplicitous friends, tried to get close to him, either directly or through my aunt Zizi, the easy-to-identify weak link. Within the family—who were increasingly concerned that the bounty was at risk—these men were known only by their surnames.

My great-uncle entrusted his money to charlatans.

One of them, the most rapacious, netted most of his fortune. History was repeating itself, this time to Raphaël's detriment. His new lover, thirty years his junior, managed to persuade Raphaël to let him take over managing the apartments.

Pleading his cause, he talked wistfully about the place he was born, like a vanished image, extolling the charms of the Midi, their second home, the place they had first met. *Chez nous.*

He was the silver-tongued director of a company that built low-cost housing: As head of "the world's biggest construction company," he talked about being on the cusp of a "new era." He would build everything, fix everything, make everything profitable. But he needed cash up front. "I shall help you, my boy," said Raphaël, laying a hand on the builder's forearm. The years of easy money were about to return. Chez nous. Inevitably, the charlatan went bankrupt, triggering fury in the family. A lawsuit followed. Raphaël received a small annuity, but the apartments were lost. In the early 1990s, the charlatan, by then in his early fifties, died of AIDS.

For Raphaël, this was a period of devastation in human terms. For the more pragmatic Lucie, it was the loss of material wealth that was the catastrophe. Raphaël lost his fortune because his flesh was weak. His lover of the moment had won him over, then taken everything. Lucie was enraged: the blackmail letter was useless now, and all her efforts to pull off her grand twofold plan—the whitewashing of the family and the enrichment of her descendants—had come to nothing.

She fantasized about every possible reprisal, including chemical castration for her uncle.

All things considered, if the apartments were irretrievably lost, there was still plenty to skim off. There was Raphaël's apartment, the country houses, the furniture, and the bank accounts, all saved from disaster. Lucie was going to have to lower her expectations and adapt her strategy. Especially since Raphaël continued his lavish spending, sometimes out of pure generosity, sometimes in a spirit of romantic optimism, as in his youth, except that now he was the one who was paying. If you liked something and my great-uncle noticed, he would give it to you: "Have it, it's yours." The recipient, whatever his relationship with the giver, would cheerfully walk off with the gift. Its value was irrelevant.

Lucie was much trickier when it came to gifts; she gave the same thing at least twice to multiple different people, who were always left deeply embarrassed. She would give, then take back—unfortunately failing to inform the original recipient—then offer the same object to a different person, taking jubilant pleasure in being thanked, and leaving the multiple recipients confused and upset. She always feigned surprise when she was unmasked. To extricate herself, she would quote, not entirely convincingly, the relevant article from the civil code: "In the case of movable property, possession is equivalent to title."

My great-uncle and my mother were like the two faces of the Roman god Janus. On the one face, the object burns your fingers like a hot potato, and it will eventually be better to get rid of it, until the last person to give it assumes his responsibility as the owner of an ill-gotten possession. On the other face, the gift was never truly a gift, as if, in an infinite process, its multiple recipients diluted my mother's responsibility.

On the whole, Raphaël was actually rather cautious; he owned no great master paintings or designer furniture that could be easily identified, though he did have a weakness for sculpture. "This is a Carpeaux," he would say proudly, avoiding saying, "This nude," or "This is the *Wounded Cupid*." He could be oddly prudish.

He lived on into his nineties, to the end of the twentieth century, remaining in his apartment for more than half a century after the Nazi spoliation.

A few weeks after his death, I received a letter from a notary inviting me to the apartment to pick up something he had left me in his will. When I arrived, the apartment had been almost emptied. People I didn't know were wandering around, unscrewing this and taking that. The place looked like it had been ransacked. There were a few paintings propped up against a wall, leaving dark rectangles on the burlap wall covering where they and others had been taken down. Even the famous whore's bed, which I used to sleep on occasionally when I stayed the night, had disappeared. Without knowing any details, I wondered if the original looting by the Nazis had taken place in the same way. Whatever the circumstances, vultures always circle in the same direction.

The notary, who looked like a Rabelaisian ogre, was seated at a makeshift trestle table alongside the assessor. I signed a receipt for the two items I had been bequeathed, and left.

I only recently learned what had happened: My mother had a spare set of keys to Raphaël's apartment, including the one to his safe. When she heard he had died, she went over with my siblings, opened the door, and declared sourly, "Help yourselves!" The implication was that there was nothing of any value left to take. So everyone helped themselves, and then my mother locked the front door behind her. Raphaël's last lover was dismissed. My cousin Hedy, who was dealing with probate, let the young man keep the car.

In his youth, Raphaël had been spurned by the family for his lifestyle; they thought him not fit to be seen with, and he had always been kept at a respectable distance, though not so distant that he would forget to write them into his will. Crowned owner of the apartment buildings after his lover's death, he became socially acceptable again.

Raphaël was not only hedonistic. He was beyond control, and that made him dangerous. Though he was never arrested for the letter, there was fear that he might attract untoward attention that would shine a light on the family's veiled history, and Lucie, always so good at keeping the rest of the family in line, had limited leverage over him. As far as she was concerned, he had caused her a lot of trouble for nothing.

My great-uncle and his niece never spoke the same language. Raphaël despised the fact that Lucie had missed out on so much. In his opinion, even her antisemitism wasn't useful. Yes, she was very bright; she could even be described as the family idealogue, but he thought she was too idealistic, not sufficiently venal. As far as he was concerned, she was a bit of a silly goose, looking for love instead of prosperity. And from a financial point of view, her antisemitism had been a failure. She had not managed to make a cent out of it.

It wasn't that Raphaël was particularly interested in fascist ideology. He was an antisemite, though he always said that everyone had been forced to collaborate. But he had made money through his relationships with Nazis simply because they were the ones in power. He might have failed his *baccalauréat*, but he had been savvy enough to know which way the wind was blowing. He would have done the same whoever was in power. It was as though he was telling his niece, "You're so clever, with all your degrees, but you haven't been a success." He focused his criticism on Lucie rather than her sister, Zizi, who made a lot of noise but had nothing like the same capabilities. It was Lucie who was a genuine rival.

Whenever the conversation turned to the period of the Occupation, Raphaël, who probably wasn't good at arguing, while also being fully aware of how opportunistic he had been, was quick to anger. "What does it matter if something is true or false if you believe it to be true? Who has right on their side?" he said, refusing to concede his own complicity. That was all he would say. Lately, he had become obsessed with the idea that "the French" weren't getting enough work. Why weren't French singers, French directors, and French producers being hired? What was it with all those singers who were impossible to understand? He was a homosexual who preached casual fascism, without properly understanding its dangers, and certainly not realizing that he might be one of its scapegoats. He refused to vote. Really, who had right on their side? Life had always been a bit of a game for him. But Lucie knew too much about him.

On the rare occasions when Raphaël did get together with the family, the unbreachable chasm between them seemed to only expand. There was one occasion when, as they sat listening in dismayed silence, he recounted how he had paid a boy he had met on a bench on the Grands Boulevards to go with him to a show, and offered more, if they got on; how later in the evening he had lost his keys and all the possessions he had on him, no doubt stolen by the boy; how he had spent the night in the hotel opposite his apartment, before he could send for the locksmith in the morning.

They seemed to find it hard to digest their Sunday roast as they listened to him recounting his amusing anecdote on the Lord's Day. *Honestly, homosexuals really ought to try to be more discreet.*

His last lover was sixty years younger than he was. It was no longer Raphaël who was the gigolo. The man who had once so loved driving his shiny blue Panhard Tigre Cabriolet that looked like a cute little toy now drove his lovers around in a Renault Clio.

But life was a party, so why worry about tomorrow? In winter, Raphaël entertained guests in his large Parisian apartment, and then, when the weather turned fine, at his weekend house, aided by my old nanny, Eugénie. In the height of summer, he welcomed guests to his old stone farmhouse in Provence. He worked hard during the festival, but what fabulous receptions in the surrounding châteaux, at the homes of charming and, more importantly, titled women. What a splendid life it was. During the day, he went into town, did a bit of shopping, met up with friends for a drink at the café by the moss-covered fountain. Then it was back to the house for a cup of Fauchon specialty tea, served at the large marble table in the shade of the hundred-year-old plane trees, before another game of *"Pédéraste et Médisante"* on the crunchy, polished white pebbles beneath the spreading mulberry tree, to the song of the cicadas.

Was the way he peppered his conversation with the names of acquaintances or people he had worked with, ostentatiously emphasizing their Jewish-sounding surnames, his way of trying to pull the wool over everyone's eyes?

He seemed to believe he had had legitimate scores to settle with the Jews. In his eyes, Vichy had done the right thing by abolishing the "appalling" Crémieux Decree that gave the Jews of Algeria French citizenship. What was that about everyone having the same rights? What a baroque notion.

I never once heard my great-uncle mention the existence of the concentration camp at Les Milles, though it was not far from the old stone farmhouse. Truly, Mozart really did erase everything.

Some mornings, after a few phone calls with "the tarts," when Raphaël could do nothing but think about the consequences if the letter were to get out, he would sit in his silk dressing gown, elbows on his knees, staring into the void, muttering a Chinese proverb: "If you sit by the river long enough, you'll see the body of your enemy float by." But the vengeance he summoned never arrived, and in any case, where would it have come from?

He thought about *Don Giovanni*, an opera he had put on too many times to count. It was as if the statue of the

Commander had come for him in person, with no Leporello there to dissuade him. If he tried to dig deeper, to get information or advice, it would mean talking about it, and that would be taking a serious risk. He was at the height of his glory and, as the Latin adage has it, the Tarpeian Rock is not far from the Capitol. A fall from grace can come swiftly and at any moment.

Lucie had acted with intelligence and skill. She turned out to be his new kindred spirit, but rather more malevolent than the first. She was going to make him pay for what he had never paid for. Raphaël, a pleasure seeker and aesthete, had always lived in the moment, never anticipating anything. He grew increasingly afraid of his niece, for my mother had him in her grip, like someone expecting a percentage in a risky business deal and prepared for the possibility of being implicated too. If Raphaël fell, there was a risk that she would too, but, as she put it, "It's worth the risk."

My mother could make Raphaël quake with no more than a glance or an allusion. He knew where he stood. No matter how he tried to soften her up with a joke—"They're my nieces, and I'm their giddy aunt!"—he trembled in her presence, because Lucie had no sense of humor. What was more, she had no ear for music. With no music and no voice, it was impossible to bend her will. This was too much for Raphaël, who was used to being able to make anyone—literally—sing for his supper.

This was a side of Lucie I didn't know. As she argued bitterly on the phone with her uncle, I could barely recognize her voice. I pictured her, in her jodhpurs, like Leni Riefenstahl, beating her high leather boots with a riding crop, flipping back a lock of hair.

Sometimes I heard her muttering under her breath about her classmates from school, all the Biancas, Simones, Dinahs, and the rest, where had they ended up, those twenty-two girls? "I can still hear their names being called in alphabetical order. I counted." It wasn't complicated: "It was only the stupid ones who were deported. You just needed a bit of cunning to find a way to slip through the net." Gone was little Lucie, with her country accent that the whole class mocked her for.

Now Raphaël's possessions belonged to the family by law. They had to be returned to them. It was only right. Raphaël had never taken her seriously. Now he would see how things were going to turn out.

Raphaël became the "Jew" of the family. Lucie had her revenge at last. My great-uncle continued to spend Sunday and Christmas alone. "Family is very important, you know. People are happy to be with each other. Or at least that's how it ought to be," he used to say to me, sitting in his armchair, never quite able to convince himself.

There were critical episodes, acute phases, brief breakups, false reconciliations, dormant periods, scenes, muted threats, telephone calls that ended abruptly, but in the end, he did more or less what she told him to. It was like a kind of endlessly disappointed love. Lucie the brave didn't feel appreciated for who she was. Raphaël the invincible felt vulnerable but now recognized her as an equal.

My mother got largely what she wanted. Not everything, of course. She took nothing for herself: Everything was to go to her children and her niece. Over time she increased the pressure, forcing Raphaël either to give away his property, or to sell it as a fictitious life annuity, or to agree to some complex legal arrangement—her law studies helped her come up with devious schemes. Her tax arrangements left the family notary perplexed, if admiring. "Your mother is quite something," he told me. They discussed the possibility of a long lease lasting ninety-nine years, which dramatically reduced the value of a property—something that in practice was no longer done—or bare ownership with right of use, which was more common. At one point someone floated the idea of Zizi marrying her uncle Raphaël to facilitate the inheritance.

Of course, Raphaël tried to get around my mother. He started giving away more and more furniture and valuables, thereby reducing the amount he "owed" my mother. As a result, she was forced to concentrate her *Aktion*, her own expropriation, on the Paris apartment, the country houses, and their contents. Everything went according to plan. The properties were sold or transferred to us at a price well below their market value, which in turn bore little relation to their cost, which was almost nothing.

Lucie seemed rational, but everything about her was threatening. In a confident tone, she told the family, "I got you out of trouble, you'd do well to remember that. We didn't do too badly in the end. We didn't lose everything. Can you imagine having your head shaved and being paraded around the city? As for you, Raphaël, Pétain didn't like pederasts, as you well know.

"And me, I'm fed up with this life—keeping house, looking after children, I don't care for any of it. I'm sick and tired of making soup, roasts, and béchamel sauce. I seem so sensible, but I did all this for you. Thanks to me we have all been quietly forgotten, and now it's gone away. So don't go telling tales, or the whole thing will never end."

Raphaël might have complained about his dispossession, but the gynaeceum was in a state of turmoil too. In secret, each of the women took turns calling Rafi, spending long hours trying to calm his anxiety.

"You know Lucie, her bark is worse than her bite," one of them would say.

"She'll never do it," another one reassured him.

"Even so, you really should think about the future," said the first.

But they were afraid of my mother too. What would have become of them without their savior? The one thing they didn't know how to do was keep going in today's world.

Raphaël died almost ruined. My family fought over what was left—and hated one another, of course, as if they hadn't been through enough.

The others got what was left. Crumbs. But is it true that you are what you own? And when you make that kind of evaluation, what does that make you?

Today after several other deaths in the family—though, of course, one can always refuse an inheritance—I own some of Raphaël's stolen objects. Beautiful things, some of which seem to have come from the pillaging of all Europe, not just Vichy France. Wanting to defy metempsychosis, I hoped that these relics, which exude terrible memories but also other, happier times in my own life, would attain a certain degree of neutrality in my home, but that would be to forget that I am a historian, specializing in World War II and the French collaboration. These objects are mine only for temporary safekeeping, and I find it almost unbearable to have them in my house. I have only to stumble upon an old key at the back of a drawer to wonder about the person who left it there.

I gave away a few things, in particular a gold reticule (which Raphaël called "my ridicule") to one of his old lovers, who had inherited nothing after my great-uncle's death. He was pleased.

My mother, who always claimed she was unable to play games, turned out to be a perfect blackmailer. The terror the very idea of the letter inspired in Raphaël was such that there was no need ever to name it. The merest hint was enough: "You know exactly what I'm talking about."

5

ON THE EVENING of August 22nd, 1944, Lucie summoned everybody to her apartment.

Three days earlier, the Paris prefecture of police had been taken over by the *Fifis*, the nickname given to the *Forces françaises de l'intérieur*, the French liberating army. In a matter of hours or days, Paris would be invaded by the Allies and the Free French. For anyone who had supported the regime that was about to tumble, it was crucial to get organized.

They all came. Without exception. Friends and relatives arrived in serried ranks. The entire clan was reunited in full force in Lucie and Friedrich's apartment on the Place des Pyramides.

Twelve people, like the twelve apostles, sitting facing their condottiere: Lucie's four childhood friends, and her family: her parents, pregnant sister Zizi with her husband, her uncle Raphaël and his lover, and last of all, the other uncle, Gaston, who had come with his niece, newly engaged to "Henriot's son." No one could work out which Henriot it was.

Only Friedrich wasn't there.

They had not been getting along.

Lucie, still only twenty-four, had adopted a way of speaking that echoed that of Goebbels: fanatical and fervent, yet restrained. Any opportunity to speak, however minor, was envisaged as an event of extraordinary dramatic intensity, with an atmosphere between trance and ecstasy. It had become her way of being. She had to galvanize people. Not convince but arouse, electrify her audience.

Lately, going into work, she had sensed the tension mounting. Teams were shrinking. People were sorting documents to be destroyed and burning them. There was the smell of downfall in the air.

It was a hot and sultry day. A storm was brewing. Lucie stood and began to address the silent group as if she were a battle commander.

"In two or three days' time, the Americans will be at the gates of Paris. There will be fierce fighting, but nothing will prevent them recapturing the city. I've heard dreadful rumors about civilians. It is total chaos.

"Now listen to me carefully, because I'm not going to say this twice. Thanks to you, I have wasted my life, my youth, and my beauty. You all went too far. You compromised yourselves. You didn't listen to me. Face facts: since the beginning everyone has seen pictures of you, everywhere, out on the town, like a bunch of dissolutes, fools, imbeciles."

She raised her fists to her temples and shook them like a pasionaria. What a strange thing, to blame everyone else for her own behavior. She may not have been photographed or filmed, but that didn't make her involvement any less significant: she was not a subject of the propaganda machine; she was the propaganda machine.

Her father sat stiffly on his stool. He didn't think he had any reason to be ashamed. He had always been a socialist, not a communist; most of his comrades from the Great War—whom he still met up with for the occasional bountiful meal—were butchers. Those dinners were where he sometimes saw Joseph Darnand, his comrade in arms in the trenches. They had the same country accent, the way they rolled their *r*'s and swallowed their syllables. They respected each other. They talked about Verdun. The Chemin des Dames. True, his old comrade was head of the *Milice* now, but it wasn't as if he had ever been involved with that lot. They wore their berets on the other side of their heads! It wasn't complicated: *miliciens* tilted their caps to the left like Alpine hunters. Not exactly what you call a patriot's beret, that's for sure.

I remember when I was little, catching glimpses of old, jagged-edged black-and-white photographs of young men wearing dark berets tilted to one side. My mother assured me—not that I asked—that they were Alpine hunters.

My grandfather hadn't joined the Waffen-SS. Everyone knew he didn't like the Krauts.

"We weren't going to let those bastards invade France!"

But he hated Jews more, not that there were many to begin with in his Burgundy village, true, and lately he hadn't seen any at all. He did think that over the past year the *Milice* had taken the bull by the horns. They'd done what needed to be done. They'd showed some action, damn it! My grandfather, a little lance corporal, had been decorated by Pétain, the hero of Verdun. And yes, he'd been brave. And now people wanted to pick a fight with him?

He had flirted a bit with those far-right fanatics from La Cagoule, because of the manager of the bank where he worked.

Lucie's father had saved the man's life during the exodus from Paris in June 1940, and the manager had always been grateful to him. They weren't from quite the same background, but the man had given him a job in "his" bank; well, he'd started in the basement, in securities, but he'd worked his way up. He liked to show off the l'Oréal coupons he bought. He owed it to Eugène Schueller, the l'Oréal founder. It was he who'd financed La Cagoule, after all.

Years later, it proved problematic for my grandfather to get himself awarded the *Légion d'honneur*, France's highest order of merit. My grandmother Herminette put pressure on Lucie, and he did, in the end, receive it. As usual, I was the messenger, carrying their correspondence, scrawled on scraps of cardboard torn from packets of melba toast, from one apartment to the other. "If he doesn't get it, do not even think of setting foot in my house ever again," Herminette wrote. My mother wept. Would my grandfather wear the ribbon instead of the rosette?

Once again, my father sighed, grumbled, and eventually did as Lucie asked. She always knew how to get what she wanted.

Lucie's father stared at his daughter. He had always criticized how she lived. He thought she was decadent. Work, family, and patriotism—those were the values of France, and her dissolute lifestyle was not going to help her achieve them. He had never forgotten how, after having volunteered in September 1939, been taken prisoner in 1940, and sent to a stalag, Lucie had not even been there that evening the following year when he had returned from captivity, having been freed because he was head of the family, all thanks to his cousin Gaston. From Herminette's flustered explanations, he eventually understood that his daughter was spending the night elsewhere. How badly she had turned out. To think he had fought in two wars for *that*.

He barely recognized his daughter in the foyer, with her hair dyed blond and dressed up to the nines. He flew into a rage; he couldn't help himself. She may have been legally an adult, but he gave her a proper piece of his mind anyway. So it was true what people were saying: She was fooling around with a German in the village, and not just any German; he was from the *Kommandantur*, a lieutenant who rode horses! Her officer was in a cavalry regiment. He'd even taught her to ride, and to speak his Kraut language. Coco Chanel was one thing. Everyone knew about Arletty, but Lucie! Did she do it just to provoke him?

Lucie never told him anything about this German from the *Kommandantur*; he never even knew his name. He must have been from northern Germany. They like horses up there.

They'd done plenty of rolling in the hay up at the stables, which didn't go unnoticed by the locals peeking through the gaps in their shutters. Shall I see you home, let me see you home, the clatter of hooves in the night and the full moon keeping watch. When the handsome rider was transferred, he left her the horse as a gift. A Nazi horse. Lucie's father sold it when he returned from captivity.

Then she found consolation with Friedrich, her young man from Alsace, who had lately started calling himself Frédéric to sound less German, not that that fooled anyone; it would be hard to find a blonder, taller, more athletic man with such blue eyes. As for his ideas! Well. Since there was no question of his daughter living in sin, Lucie's father had made them get married, to silence the rumors, sanctified by a "Jewish pebble," a diamond ring that Raphaël had somehow got hold of that fit her finger perfectly, like her new life. At least it had been an opportunity for a lavish black market feast with the family.

Lucie's father coughed lightly. Ever since being gassed in the trenches he had suffered from shortness of breath.

Lucie began with her sister.

"Zizi, do you have even two pennies' worth of common sense? What was this obsession with being in the double page spread of *Signal*? 'A reception at the embassy'! What about this headline: 'A beautiful, veiled mystery woman, in a fascinator and a white organdie dress.' You may not have been named in the caption, but it's not as if everyone didn't know it was you. They even told me about it at the bakery. Don't you have anything better to do with your time instead of pampering yourself all day long? Just look at you, with your miserable face."

Zizi let out a whimper and shifted her buttocks in her chair as if trying to hide her discomfort. She dabbed her eyes affectedly with her handkerchief. Lately she had been on edge, sometimes bursting into tears for no reason. Things were not going well with her husband, who was constantly away visiting "friends." She was twenty-two, but already her heavy legs were painful; she should have been out stretching them in this heat. Her skin was blotchy from the pregnancy, and she was still three months away from her due date. She threw a sidelong glance at her husband, who pretended not to notice. She swore this child would be her first and last. She was not cut out to be a mother.

She looked down at her cuticles and silently pushed them back with her fingernail. How had she ended up like this? Early on in the Occupation her uncle Raphaël had told her she ought to sing, she had such a lovely voice. He even offered her private lessons with a famous teacher. But you have to work at it, it's terribly tiring, and a light, breathy voice wouldn't cut it.

Through a friend, Zizi had found herself a job as an assistant in a boutique that served a certain type of petit bourgeois woman, more posturing than poised; the clothes were always a little too snug, which made them extra demanding, taking it out on the hemline or grousing about a button.

She went to acting classes with the gang and her friend Rosita, who called herself Corinne to sound chic, as if Corinne sounded chic! Rosita, who also called herself Zizi, seemed to have everything going for her, but this peroxide-blond good-time girl was clearly a little lost. She was mother to little Brigitte, whose father was a German airman. At least the child's name was spelled the same in French and German and easy to remember.

Anyway, Zizi was very happy to be married. She had no idea yet what she was going to call the baby. In any case, she was going to hand it over to her parents to take care of. She didn't see herself bringing up a child at twenty-two.

Now it was time for Lucie's friends. The foursome sat in a row by the half-open window, trying to get some fresh air. They looked at her, their gazes level.

"Oh, you lot, with your pathetic made-up names. Seriously, do you take everyone for idiots? Pierrette, Josette, Suzette, Zouzou... surely you could have come up with something a bit more imaginative. How about Blanchette, while you're at it?"

No one laughed. They weren't what you would call well educated, but they all knew the fate of Monsieur Seguin's goat. They sat apprehensively waiting for what came next, watching their Lucie, with her sardonic smile and her long nose, who always managed to wrap everyone around her little finger. She was the only one of them who had a proper education; the friends had only their school certificates when they were twelve. At the age of twenty, all four had gone in search of pastures new. They moved to Paris with nothing but their bodies and their youth, and no time to lose. Fifteen years down the road it would be too late.

Lucie would never let them down. She had not forgotten where she came from, like them.

Zouzou was the daughter of a neighborhood washerwoman in Paris; her mother did laundry for the occupying forces, who didn't have their own cleaning service. Zouzou was tall and lanky, with a slightly horsey face, a superb figure, and lustrous auburn hair. She was always impeccably turned out in jackets nipped in at the waist and starched and ironed by her mother. She was about to be married, though her betrothed was not always amenable and could have done with being a wee bit taller. But now was not the time to be demanding. She had to put behind her the attempted suicide with an overdose of barbiturates after her surgeon boyfriend ditched her for the boss's daughter. She still hadn't really got over it.

Because she was by nature melancholy and had absolutely no taste, Zouzou later turned to ready-to-wear, then interior design; by the 1970s she was proposing leopard skin wallpaper to her clients, who simply adored it. Ah, Zouzou! She had an innate sense of what was about to be all the rage, even going so far as to suggest sexy mirrors on the ceiling as a change from boring old *toile de Jouy*. She tried the look out in her own little apartment, and the effect was marvelous. You had to know how to surprise the ladies, and their husbands even more.

Zouzou had already designed her storefront. Her name would unfurl across the whole length of it, along with the word *Décoration*. Cushions embroidered with her monogram. Avenue Marceau or nothing. She had spotted a space that had been empty for a while. At the opening party, she'd have some little filly in a white apron serve champagne to guests deep in conversation about the various merits of the fireplace nook and the love seat.

Who was it who had called her a kept woman the other day? What was wrong with a demimondaine? Even midinette would have been nicer. Zouzou was trying to learn to speak chic for her customers, the plummy accent cultivated in the fancy Parisian neighborhood of Ranelagh, as if she had a hot chestnut in her mouth. Speak slowly, with a gravelly voice, clearly enunciating the last syllable of each word. Stand up straight, feet slightly turned out. Wear flat heels so as not to look even taller. Chin up, like a dancer or, better still, a movie actress. She had seen it in a magazine.

Lucie would get her out of this. She was always able to figure things out. What a swell girl. They should let her have her say.

Josette's mind was wandering, but she could tell Lucie was furious. She was really going for it. Actually, Josette was her name—well, her fourth middle name, after the first three that sounded, in order, like a virgin (Mary), a nun (Anne), and a saint (Thérèse). Not quite her style. Since she had begun an affair with a nice young chap with a hospital named after him, Josette was also making plans to get married. Madame the Doctor was her dream. And she went to so much trouble, gave so much of herself, that when her surgeon was on call, their noisy lovemaking became a matter of public record. She was like that, Josette, hot-blooded, and nature had been generous; she had considerable assets that she put to excellent use. A body is meant to be pampered, she told herself, as she flaunted her generous bosom in a black push-up brassiere (men love black lingerie). Her brown hair was styled like her heroine Ava Gardner, her olive complexion was tanned all year round, her subtle epilation left her skin perfectly smooth, and her mouth was carmine, the color maintained by the repeated application, under the gaze of an admirer, of lipstick drawn slightly over the lip line. A long cigarette with a white filter dangled from her lips, moving in time with her chatter, and her hoarse smoker's voice was alluring. She was romantic. Not sweet, romantic. She wasn't stunning, but she was extremely likeable.

She didn't understand why her lover insisted that "afterward" they should move into the Gestapo house in the next town. Of course, it was a beautiful plush villa surrounded by a large garden, a little out of the way, and it was available, but only because no one else wanted to live there . . . Well, soon she would have a new surname. Lord God, *Herrgott*, what a surname! No more Alsace; farewell, Papa. Enough was enough. Her body had always taken her wherever she wanted to go.

Then there was Suzette, with her dreamy expression, still pursuing ambitious projects despite a recent setback. No

Madame Everyman, she had already embroidered her wedding trousseau with the intertwined initials of her chosen one, an aristocrat with a double-barreled name. But then it all fell apart. Just thinking about it, the humiliation! He came back one evening from his parents' house. He had been planning to tell them everything. He began by calling her Suzanne, in a somber tone of voice, something he had never done before. Bad start. She was a fine young woman—that could mean anything. Suzette could only remember bits and pieces of what he'd said: "A question of principles... One has a status to maintain... A young lady from a good family." He had been told in no uncertain terms that an aristocrat must marry an aristocrat.

To think she had almost made it.

But Suzette also knew it would be hard to find a more fetching and cheerful woman in such excellent health, with a callipygous rump that was an open invitation to hanky-panky, as her aristocrat liked to tell her. Now she was seeing an official from the Commissariat-General for Jewish Affairs. A pleasant enough chap, not particularly chatty or curious, a serious type who wanted to settle down and start a family. He wouldn't pull any tricks on her. Of course, there was no barony attached, but the Jewish question is a serious business. Suzette was a good cook, and she pictured herself entertaining with her husband and decorating their weekend house. Being a homemaker was an excellent prospect. It had status. And then when he was done with the Jewish question, or even if he carried on with it, their future would be all about faith, the mantilla, the church of Saint-Nicolas-du-Chardonnet, the Latin mass, novenas, and pilgrimages. She would make sure all memory of her previous life was erased. She would see to it that decorum was respected. Of course, the good Lord knew, but he wouldn't talk.

That left Pierrette at the end of the row. The least gifted and most insecure of them all, stodgy and slow, she was trying but failing to follow what Lucie was saying. She cleared her throat. She had been born Petra but preferred her Frenchified name; the Serbs might use the Cyrillic alphabet, but everyone knew that some of them were friends with the Nazis. How was she ever going to get through this? Imagine marrying someone from the Resistance! The bespectacled aviator type, a cadet in the Free France movement, full of his brave exploits, but humble. How dull! Well, she shouldn't exaggerate. But still.

Anyway, let's see what Lucie has to say. She would help get her out of this fix. She would get them all out of this fix. But what was with this tone of voice?

The four friends peered up at Lucie through their eyelashes. Had she forgotten where she came from? And she'd had plenty of nicknames too, Luzia, Lucia, Lucy, or had they invented them? She'd better not go pretending it was Hungarian. Granted, a lot of countries had joined the Axis, but still. How she had banged on about that name: *Lucie!* Light. Except her life was anything but a fairy tale.

She was a smart young lady, Lucie, who knew exactly

what she was doing, though she pushed it sometimes with her outfits, like that time she turned up at the doctor's office in a pair of riding boots and he asked her, "Do you ride?" and she replied, quick as a flash, "Yes, every morning at seven a.m." Well, it could have been true.

But she mustn't get distracted. It was the family's turn.

"*You*," she said, turning to her sister's husband. "No more doing business with the Germans, no more sending fur-lined gloves to the Russian front. Couldn't you have found something better to do? Monsieur Mittens, off you trot!"

Monsieur Mittens threw his sister-in-law a sidelong glance. She always used to be so cheerful when he took her out for a spin in his Bugatti. Peroxide blond, like a picture-perfect German girl. More authentic than the real thing. Once a Nazi, always a Nazi. They'd be wise to keep their mouths shut, she and her Friedrich. Things could turn out badly for them.

And what if he did have an alias? Everyone in business had an alias. Even if the business was gloves. There is no such thing as a stupid way of making a living. Monsieur Mittens was not the first and he wouldn't be the last to have a procurement office. As for that fancy expression *black market*! But perhaps he would have been better off buying a bar.

Anyhow, he'd had it with all these crazy women. His wife, Zizi, had become a total bore almost overnight. Obsessively fussy in domestic matters, always picking fights, manically clearing and cleaning up.

Lucie turned to her uncle.

"Raphaël, what on earth were you thinking? Did you really believe your German was going to protect you? Well, he has no one to protect him now. You do realize that everybody recognized you on the newsreel the other day at the movie theater? Oh sure, the auditorium may have been lit up to stop people hissing, but as I expect you noticed, everyone hissed anyway. It was really not very clever of you. Now you're the first person that comes to mind whenever anyone mentions Mozart. You know what people call you? Widow Mozart! Which I don't find remotely amusing.

"They were photographed, you were caught on film. That was a huge risk to take. And given all your antics, someone, someday, is bound to talk. Ah! How handsome he was, your German. But he's gone now. They've all gone. We're on our own now."

Raphaël was running out of patience. "How about your *Oraff*, is that a French company?" he muttered under his breath. The *Office de répartition de l'affichage. Oraff.* However you say it, Orlaff, Orloff, Oralf, Orff, Carl Orff, it all sounded suspiciously German. A name like that, it's like the mark of Cain. Was Lucie blind? She was starting to be a worry. A true fanatic. Did she think they were going to get away with it?

It was quite obvious really: Lucie was one of those women who were never wrong and even less likely to admit it if they were.

Lucie turned to Uncle Gaston, who was, in fact, not her uncle but her father's first cousin.

With his legs crossed at the ankle, his bow tie straight, Gaston appeared relaxed as he drew on his briar pipe. What was Lucie going on about? What a mess. It was quite inappropriate for her to lecture him. He had trained her, after all.

She looked at him without speaking.

None of this would be enough to stop the great reversal of fortune that was taking place.

Lucie turned from Gaston to her cousin, who sat staring at her. The future Madame Henriot Junior appeared to have no idea that times had changed. Admittedly, her husband-to-be was not the son of the famous Henriot that everyone was always talking about, but that was just a detail. It seemed as if Lucie, deliberately or not—you never knew with her—was also fueling the misunderstanding. Presumably it suited her.

"We cannot be seen to socialize with the Henriots anymore. And you, with your name, are too close to them. We have to think of ourselves. From now on, we are distant relatives who see each other only at weddings and funerals. All of you, when you think 'Henriot,' say 'Henri.' It's not difficult. Henri is fine."

The younger Henriot's fiancée listened, her face pale. Her Henriot was not the son of the great Philippe. She no doubt wished he were, but one can't have everything. Her thoughts began to drift. She'd seen a photograph in *Signal* of Philippe Henriot's son sitting with his dog between his legs. Apparently, since the annexation of Alsace, the name *wolfhound* had been replaced by *German shepherd*. This kind of thing had always gone on with the Germans and the Alsatians. But surely a dog is just a dog.

Lucie stopped speaking and took a sip of water. They sat and watched her. The cold water seemed to do her good. It seemed to be helping her gather her thoughts.

"We are no longer conquering heroes. Now those idiots are swanning around like they own the place. They call themselves the Resistance, but what are they resisting? You tell me. Everyone did what we did. But then a few smart alecks saw the wind changing. The rest are just a bunch of cowards.

"We believed, and we still do. This is how things are now. Our enemies are the same, but now we shall have to be discreet. It's a setback. We must let this first wave pass. It will take time. But all is not lost. I can't say more than that.

"In the meantime, we'll have to fend for ourselves. You will all do exactly what I tell you. First of all, burn everything. Don't throw things away, burn them."

"Even our copies of *Signal*?" said Zizi, aghast.

"You can keep a few. Everyone reads magazines. But burn any letters that mention us. Straightaway. This is no time for sentiment.

"Watch what comes out of your mouth. Never mention the past. Stick to small talk with friends and neighbors.

"Have you got that? If you help someone, you compromise

yourself. So, no helping each other anymore. And if I catch you at it, you'll have me to answer to."

She took a deep breath. "I wish I didn't have to say this, but we are going underground. No one is ever to utter a word of German. We have never spoken German."

Everyone nodded. It was true; German had never been their strong point—except for Lucie, of course.

"If by some chance you do let slip a German word, just say it's Alsatian. I'll give you a tip: whenever you find yourself thinking 'German,' say to yourself 'Italian' instead. Instead of 'Hitler,' say 'Mussolini.' Instead of 'the Führer', say 'Il Duce.' It means the same thing. *Duce* means *Führer*. The word Nazi has no particular significance for you. Anyway, all that was in Germany. If you can't help it, try *fascist*. A fascist carries fasces or a bundle of rods; it's a kind of Italian Olympic sport. Never use the word *collaboration* or *collaborator*. Just say 'works with.' It means the same thing. Every time you think the word 'Aryan,' say 'Celt' instead. And most importantly of all, never, ever talk about the Jews. Never, ever use that word."

They were beginning to wonder if they should be taking notes.

"What about the Maréchal?" one of her friends ventured. Lucie hesitated for a moment. That was a big subject.

"You can talk about Pétain from time to time. He did fight at Verdun after all.

"Anyway, I hope you've all got it: you can only talk about Italy. Exaggerate your pronunciation, wave your hands around, say, '*Allora, ma che ci faccio? Ma che dico?*'" (Lucie spoke much better German than Italian.) "And if anyone asks you something specific, pretend you don't understand. We all argue all the time anyway. We're practically Neapolitan. Italians absolutely adore drama. And don't forget: we eat polenta."

At this point someone spoke up. "Yes, polenta is Italian, but they eat it in the north, in Piedmont. You know, where your German friends dreamed of transferring the population to Burgundy, for your famous *Burgund* project. Now you're just mixing everything up. We're from Puglia. You've always told us we arrived in Algeria barefoot because we couldn't afford to buy shoes. We're from the heel of the boot, where they don't eat polenta."

Lucie was unconcerned by this detail. "Oh, just say it's a family tradition, handed down from Grand-mère Abramo."

"Lucie, you're getting it all wrong," Raphaël interjected. "Grand-mère Abramo, as you keep calling her—she was never a grandmother. I never met her. She died of tuberculosis in Algeria, when she was twenty-six, when her daughter Herminette was only four. My half-sister, sitting over there, has literally no memory of her mother. She was packed off to boarding school with the nuns, where she learned to embroider and play the piano. Your Grand-mère Abramo barely had time to be a mother, let alone a grandmother. And we have no idea if she ate polenta."

Lucie was adamant. "All the records are in Algeria. No one's going to check, I promise you. In any case, I have the family record book. Grand-mère Abramo's first name was

Maria Theresa, like the Empress. And her mother's maiden name was Waltre—in other words, Walther, typically German. She had an Alsatian accent because her Alsatian family sided with the French in the 1870 war. We definitely have German blood."

Uncle Raphaël couldn't believe his ears. "Are you referring to the Empress of Austria? She was a Habsburg! And what's all this about her accent?"

"Fine," Lucie conceded. "Marie-Thérèse spoke French. She was born south of Constantine, in a village built from scratch by French settlers. When she was nineteen, she married a man named Abramo, a farmer from Italy. So, we're French, from Algeria. I do wish you would stop interrupting the whole time."

Raphaël raised his voice. "Have you suddenly become an expert, Lucie? This is pure fiction. You should be writing novels. You do know that Abramo is a Jewish name? It's Abraham in Italian. Jewish. I'm not saying that makes us Jewish, it's passed down through the mother." Then he added, with a sly little smile, "I don't know if the rabbinate is still open, but we could ask around. There are still a few Abramos in Puglia."

Lucie ignored him. She didn't want to spoil the climax of her speech. The grand peroration was approaching. "Grand-mère Abramo is the *Ur-grossmutter* of us all." (Her pronunciation was impeccable.) "The original grandmother, the head of a great lineage, at the very apex of our family tree. She's mentioned in every family saga. All the great civilizations are matriarchies."

There was a murmur. Lucie was clearly still under Friedrich's spell. Ever since she had started dabbling in genealogy, it was impossible to argue with her. A few days earlier she had even claimed that our surname was derived from the chief of the Goths. Only she believed it.

Exhausted after all this talk in the stifling heat, everyone was now in a hurry to leave, regardless of any potential danger. But Lucie held up a hand to indicate they should remain seated. She hadn't finished yet. They still had to hear the finale, the ideological declaration.

"It is time to assume our responsibilities. Whoever remains standing after this battle, it will not be the mediocre!"

And like one of the Fates, she began to apportion out the destiny of each one.

"You, Zizi, will go to Reims, to live with your parents-in-law. They're pharmacists, so you'll be safe. No one will think to look for you there. That's where you'll give birth. Your husband will join you once he's wrapped up all his affairs. I'll come and see you as soon as I can."

Zizi groaned. "*Oh, Lu-cie!*"

Ignoring her, Lucie turned to Raphaël and his lover. "You two are to go back to the south of France. Keep a low profile. Make new friends. You like countesses; find yourself a new one. Be discreet. Only go into town to buy groceries. No socializing. You can spend your time reading and playing the piano." She gave a bitter smile. She knew she wouldn't be invited.

"You're going to go back to Les Chomettes," she said to her parents, "where everybody knows you. You'll be fine there. Maman, Burgundy is very pleasant. I know you don't like the countryside, you're afraid of mice, you hate spiders, but there's no other solution." Lucie's mother lifted her chin with a look of defiance but said nothing.

To her cousin, she said, "You can go with Uncle Gaston to the presbytery in Les Chomettes. A presbytery is always a good idea. But no socializing with Papa."

Finally, she turned to her four old friends. "As for you ladies, go home to your families. It won't be forever. We just have to wait for the storm to pass."

For once, the chorus kept its counsel.

Somberly, Lucie declared, "I shall stay in Paris with Friedrich. To maintain the family honor." No one spoke. They were too stunned. All gripped by the same dread.

Lucie had planned their survival down to the last detail.

They filed out of the apartment. She was right, of course. But what she called going underground was just a cobbled-together mess. She had obviously never tried to pull off anything like this before.

Lucie locked the front door behind her. It was going to be a lot more difficult to convince Friedrich. That very morning, a miniature casket had arrived for him in the mail, an anonymous threat from someone in the Resistance.

The escape plan was put into immediate effect. Everyone scattered like fowl to spend the rest of their lives under self-imposed house arrest. The years would add up, but at least they had been granted. They had lived through so much already. Those who went back to the village barely saw one another again, even decades after the final law granting full amnesty was passed on August 6th, 1953. *You can never be too sure.*

A small detachment made up of the ladies of the gynaeceum returned to live in Paris. They kept their counsel.

They had all lived so much already, everything that came after was drab and redundant.

One after another, people died and were buried in the small cemetery in Les Chomettes, high on the hill looking down at the village and the beautiful church that chimes the Angelus three times a day.

Saint-Florentin was never the capital of Burgundy. It was, however, the capital of a lightly salted, creamy cow's cheese that Lucie regularly, almost religiously, fed to her children and their friends.

6

AFTER THE BIRTH of her children, since she'd had it up to here with family life, Lucie started letting slip clues about her past. Some she sowed deliberately for someone to find; others were like hints to be deciphered from her dream life.

I grew up caught in the twisted loop of lies and truth. My mother read me fairy tales by Hans Christian Andersen and the brothers Grimm, and the stories of Père Castor. "Little Red Riding Hood," "Goldilocks and the Three Bears," "Marlaguette and the Wolf." She bequeathed me a lifelong love of reading, taught me how to understand the meaning of a story, how to tell it, how to conjure a story from an image.

But I also sensed in her a disturbing dissociation from reality, for she lived in a fantasy world where facts were contingent, experience was to be distrusted or ignored. This passionate Germanist played the game of *als ob*, as if. In German, *als ob* generates the hypothetical general subjunctive mood (in contrast to the special subjunctive mood, which is used to report indirect speech). The general subjunctive mood is used after a conjunction — if, would, as if it were—and thus *als ob* expresses the unreal while simultaneously, with the grammatical rigor of German, lending it a high degree of credibility. Where English would use a simple conditional—the language of a child inventing a fantasy world—with the German subjunctive mood, one remains rooted in a kind of delirium without ever returning to reality.

Lucie transposed this unreality into a French of her own invention. When we were little, she would say things like, "It *would* be like this," "We *would* do it this way," "That's how we *would* think," "*As though* Friedrich had said . . ."

Was she still caught up in the thrill of victory, consumed with the desire to reach the heights that had taken her and Friedrich so far, or was she living in another world, trying to escape reality? She must have realized she had lost everything, but she refused to accept it. All she had left was denial. Lying to oneself makes things more bearable. If one repeats a lie for long enough, eventually it becomes the truth. With Hitler, as Friedrich once wrote in a postcard to her, it was all or nothing: *Mit Hitler—Alles oder Nichts*. Which meant it had to be all, including falsehoods, compromised integrity, smoke screens, occasional venom, and a spot of duplicity dusted with propaganda. Anyone who didn't adhere to her system was cast out of her life.

My mother tossed out the odd clue here and there for us children to pick up. We didn't understand everything, but we did get the hang of certain words and phrases, and soon began to make connections. Lucie played *als ob* in every possible way, with shocking bad faith, trying to get us to play along. Some of us lost interest, and others caught on quickly, especially those of us who realized it was the only way to get her attention. Children are loyal, they adapt; they have no choice but to speak the same language as their parents, simply in order to exist.

Lucie encouraged us at breakfast by serving us oatmeal, which looks like muesli but doesn't taste like it. "One spoon for Lucie. One spoon for Friedrich." Who was Friedrich? we wondered. Lucie was interested only in who ate the oatmeal. Children who preferred bread were a burden to her. Some of us were toast children and some were oatmeal children. The toast children, who had buttered toast in the shape of butterfly wings, were Charles's children, while the porridge children, more malleable (their bowls of porridge had rims decorated with petal-shaped blobs of oatmeal drawn by Lucie to cool it down), were Friedrich's children. "One petal for Lucie. One petal for Friedrich," she would say, opening her mouth at the same time as the child. It was with the oatmeal children that she shared her painful story and her flights of *als ob*. You had to love oatmeal to be on Lucie's side.

At snack time, the ultimate treat was a hearty slice of *schmalz*: a piece of rye bread sliced with a deer horn knife and spread with lard—four clues for anyone who could decipher them. Yuck. This was what made the world coherent and everyone able to cope with Lucie's pain. Nazism was also about food.

My brother and I both began picking up clues. Short of falling sick, there was no other way of arousing our mother's interest in us. It was a straightforward choice: hospital or the general subjunctive mood, and we chose grammar rather than the sick bay. This unusual form of communication was part of the rules. But for the game to be complete, to reach the heights of the general subjunctive mood, Lucie had to be evasive, neither confirming nor denying our questions.

"Is that right, *Maman*, do you agree?"

"Yes, my little one, my baby doll, my darling Thumbelina, one might well think so."

My brother, the firstborn, was named Frédéric. He might as well have been called Friedrich Junior. Lucie liked to sweep his blond hair back and dress him in lederhosen, Austro-Bavarian leather short pants. Friedrich Junior was a dream child, in both senses: He was perfectly behaved, and he fulfilled Lucie's fantasy, though she would have far preferred for him to have been fathered by Friedrich. From an early age, he was told that he was going to study medicine and become a doctor—that he would be just like Friedrich, whose name sounded almost the same as his. In a way Lucie's hopes were fulfilled; Frédéric became a "head doctor," a clinical psychologist who spent most of his career working in psychiatric hospitals, treating former Waffen-SS men who were now doddering old men, senile old collaborators who got their wars all mixed up, and ex-soldiers destroyed by the Algerian War. Highly intelligent, he quickly grasped what was wrong with our mother and from an early age refused to be called by the name she had given him, going instead by Félix, his middle name. Frédéric contained too many ghosts.

What was there to be said about her second husband, Charles, who had allowed his wife to name his child Friedrich? He rarely gave his older son gifts, "as if" he thought he was someone else's son, a cuckoo in the nest he had built with Lucie.

At least I was not named Frieda, but I might as well have been. I can still hear Lucie's pride when she showed off how my first words as a baby were *A-Hi* and *Fa-di*, my mutilated version of my brother's name—and of the other Friedrich. As an adult, I discovered that "Ahi" was the nickname given to Hitler by his entourage: *A* for Adolf, *Hi* for Hitler. Later, at my mother's insistence, I began studying biology. But I soon gave up; I wasn't scientifically minded, and I had the feeling that it was taking me too far from who I was.

As I grew older Lucie encouraged me, praising my intelligence and my quick thinking. It didn't matter if I didn't do well at science, for German would be my intellectual sustenance. *Backen, buk, gebacken.* My mother would read the tricky passage, resting her chin on her hand, her mouth twisted into the same pout she always made for any activity requiring concentration. Repeat.

She sighed. "This is the third time I've studied German, and the third time I've forgotten it all." Another clue. One day, you will tell my story. One day, you will tell what happened. But first you have to learn about *als ob*. You are here to live somebody else's life. Remember: "It would be as if" means "that's how it was." "We would say that" means "we said that." You will have to fill in the blanks, to find the meaning, to find connections between events, beyond what was. It is your heritage, the role that has fallen to you, and it is the only role you will have.

But my questions were met with evasive answers or flat-out denials—the realm of the *als ob* did not descend into the real world. I had to cross-check, construct hypotheses. I felt like a simultaneous interpreter, and it was exhausting. It was like trying to master the general subjunctive mood when I couldn't even grasp the simple past.

Not all of us children understood at the same pace. My horrified older brother grasped it and tried to steer clear (he was already learning Latin and Greek), but he suffered his fate anyway. My older sister, co-opted by our father, was unable to serve two masters, and she aggressively protected herself from our mother. My younger brother was still a baby.

By the age of three or four, I was already frightening my school friends by relaying stories I'd heard from the gynaeceum, particularly from Herminette, my morphine-addled grandmother. The tale of a thief caught in the act who hurled at her female accuser in court: "The crowbar will cost you dearly, Mademoiselle!" I wondered who the thief was. Could it have been Herminette herself? The young girl with long braids who got on the metro and when she got off again her braids had been chopped off. Stories I got from out-of-date Occupation newspapers. I had far too much imagination. I gave my classmates nightmares, their parents complained to the teacher, my mother was summoned. I was told to stay quiet and keep my fears to myself. The crowbar would cost me dearly. It cost the young women with shaved heads dearly too.

Once Lucie took the gynaeceum to vacation in the house in Les Chomettes. Accompanied by her sister, Zizi, and her four old friends, who were all married now but came without their menfolk, my mother was relaxed and ebullient. It would be only a matter of time before she started talking with a Burgundy accent again. I sat in her lap. I was four years old, her baby doll, and I was not supposed to understand. It was summer; the cherries in the orchard were ready to be picked. Lucie had constructed a solid rural mythology, as if she and her family were happy part-time farmers, feeding themselves almost entirely with the fruits of their harvest. The reality was more prosaic: Lucie owned sixty-three trees outside an unremarkable village, through which ran a busy main road.

Once again, my mother recounted the saga of the family orchard. A certain drunken Father Marmot, from a neighboring village, had grafted one of the family's cherry trees and produced a new variety of plump delicious cherries (Lucie would never have dared use the word *resistant*). Thus was born a variety of cherries known as marmot cherries, which were soon being grown throughout the region. Everyone tried to picture this barely sentient man taking out his pocketknife and grafting the tree. Lucie told the story well and they all seemed to believe her. It was so much simpler that way.

It was only much later that I learned about a new method of grafting fruit trees that had been introduced to occupied France by the Nazis; based on Nazi theories of agriculture, it was known as "approach grafting." In this nonintrusive technique, a strip of bark is removed from both graft and rootstock. The two wounds are aligned so they are touching, then tied and covered with mastic. This was German grafting. An intermediary was brought in to teach the new method. Another kind of collaboration. You get close, as close as possible, you pass the baton, then lots of children come along. Even the trees were there to reproduce. In a way, it was the Lebensborn of cherry trees, *le temps des cerises nazies.*

Once Lucie hit her stride, she could go on telling stories for hours. There was the one about a certain Petiot and his boiler. He was born in the neighboring town; they knew him a little. It so happened that my grandfather knew Petiot's brother. In his apartment in Paris, he "burned people," took their money, their jewelry, and all the valuables they had packed in their suitcases. My grandfather had even recovered a pair of shoes from the dump near the village.

What a character he was, my grandfather. Petiot was too. He pretended to be the head of the Fly-Tox Resistance network, tricking Jews who were hoping to flee to Argentina. He went to great lengths to pull it off. But he got caught in the end. Oh, how everybody laughed.

In an old newspaper, I read about a Dr. Marcel Petiot, Rue Le Sueur in Paris. Was it the same man? My mother never said he was a doctor, but the unease persisted.

Because the atmosphere seemed right for it, Lucie began talking about Henriot, though she didn't say his first name or how we were connected. He had died "tragically." The atmosphere became less merry and more reflective.

They forgot I was there. Clutching my comfort blanket, I wriggled in my mother's lap and said, "Who is Henriot?" Lucie frowned. The laughter died away. The party was over. No one spoke. A shiver ran through the group. They had better not be betrayed by a child! My mother gathered herself, took a deep breath, and replied in a grave tone, "I did not say Henriot, I said Herriot. I was talking about the Mayor of Lyons. A politician." No one else said a word. I knew I had heard Henriot, but who was I supposed to believe? My mother or my ears? It was just one letter difference. I heard "hen," not "her," Henriot and not Herriot. I had already seen photographs of both men in old newspapers at home, where time seemed to stand still. One looked like an ox (Herriot) and one like a wolf (Henriot). And why were all the women on edge all of a sudden? Uncertainty set in that lasted for years.

I discovered dictionaries when I was a bit older, which I learned to revere. They fix the meanings of words, their spelling, and sometimes even the way they sound. But in the meantime, to whom did I owe my loyalty? I was leaning toward the wolf, like in a fairy tale, but no way was I going to tell my mother.

Lucie was panicked: I had understood, and children talk. Seized by irrational fear, she hedged and began trying harder to cover her tracks. She wanted me to know, yes, but not until I was older. At this rate, eventually the *als ob* would be useless and she would be found out. Suspicious of this child with her musical ear, she began using homonyms, speaking in rapid-fire English so that I wouldn't understand. She was trying to confuse me, and indeed I was feeling more and more bewildered. How was this word spelled? And how was it pronounced? I was becoming a nuisance. Henriot or Herriot? If it was Henriot, which one was she talking about? Philippe the orator? Or the other one? "They're homonyms," was all she would say.

It was a bit like a multiple-choice quiz, with one correct, one approximate, and one wrong response, but my mother never said what the answer was. I had to choose between Henriot (Philippe), Henriot (a different one), and Herriot. Which one was part of our family? Which one was the *als ob*? Which was the wrong one? I chanted to myself, like a litany, "Henriot, Herriot, Henriot," hoping that the truth would emerge, but the oracle remained silent. Over time, I transformed the multiple-choice quiz into a question with one right and one wrong answer. I hesitated between Henriot (Philippe) and Herriot. When my mother uttered the name of the former it was with suppressed pride.

My elder brother, meanwhile, hesitated between Henriot (the other one) and Herriot. We were divided. Family secrets were not shared.

Our mother's treasure hunt was under way, and she was jubilant. This time, she had surpassed herself.

Years later, a conversation with a curator in the archives finally helped me figure out the truth. Yes, there had indeed been two Henriot boys, one the son of the notorious secretary of state for information in the Vichy government, and one the son of a different Henriot. They were the same age, had the same surname, and both had married in 1949. My mother's cousin had drawn the short straw; she married the son of the "other" Henriot.

For decades I was on the wrong track, convinced my mother's cousin's husband was the son of the never-to-be-mentioned Philippe Henriot.

My mother, who would have so loved to add the propagandist to the family tree, had always enjoyed the ambiguity, the *als ob*. In the absence of the real Henriot, the evil genius of the Vichy propaganda machine, its veritable founding father, she had to make do with the "as if."

She fabricated and lied throughout her life and was adept at exploiting misunderstandings. She even made her own sister believe that the "Henriot son" rode motorbikes at the NSKK, the *Nationalsozialistisches Kraftfahrkorps*, the National Socialist Motor Corps, with the "real" Henriot, a claim that Zizi was quick to repeat. Yet another red herring.

Compared with this masterstroke, other misunderstandings were trifling. Was she referring to Mendel (Gregor, the geneticist of the famous laws, with his cassock and rimmed spectacles) or Mandel? (Georges Mandel was born Louis

Rothschild. He was a Jewish journalist who defended Alfred Dreyfus. A street in the neighboring arrondissement where our cousins lived, the ones we were no longer supposed to associate with, was named after him.)

Anything was possible merely by changing one letter, or even changing nothing at all. Was this person Lucie mentioned a Resistance fighter or a collaborator, a Jew or an Aryan? I started looking for clues, but I was quickly disoriented. Ultimately, it was the German language that saved me, with its precision and clarity; every letter is pronounced. There is no silent e in German.

Lucie always remained devoted to Les Chomettes. That was where she was truly happy, in the house in Burgundy that had belonged to her and Friedrich, and that would forever be a memorial to him. Down in the village, she allowed us to ride around on our little red bicycles, build shacks on the hillside, and climb the maypole (what they call in German the *Maibaum*) on holidays.

Bremen, Hamburg, Stettin; the Weser, the Elbe, and the Oder. *The recitation is over. You're free to go.* Don't ask me why you know the rivers of northern Germany so well.

In her jodhpurs and riding boots, Lucie loved to explore the area at the wheel of her 2CV with her children in the back. She acted as if she owned the place, doing just as she pleased, as she always had done, not giving a hoot about what anyone said of her. It was all heroic. If Burgundy had fulfilled its destiny as Lotharingia, Lucie would have become the local *Gauleiter*, district head. Sometimes Friedrich's nephew and niece, our cousins from Alsace, came to stay, the boy in short trousers and the girl sporting long blond braids. They were family.

"Shall we take the old Roman road? Look how straight it is, and the view's so clear. You could almost imagine seeing Caesar." Ah, the Romans and their mighty civilization. Burgundy was full of Gallo-Roman towns. And Lucie, just like Friedrich, just like every German back in the day, always wrote the month in Roman numerals, between the day and the year in Arabic numerals.

"Would you like to visit a ruined castle? Let's pretend we're thinking of buying an old tower. Or we could say we're on an archaeological dig." The past has layers like geological strata. Lucie cheerfully rewrote history to honor Friedrich's memory: According to her, all the most important popes were Germanic, and the instigators of the French Revolution too. The great artists of the Italian Renaissance were descended from Goths and Lombards.

I didn't understand everything, but I could tell how exhilarated my mother was. This was her version of *Land und Leute*, a survey of land and people. She thought she could discern in the face of some local man the features of Chancellor Rolin in the Van Eyck painting from five centuries earlier. He was Flemish, of course. The same stock.

"Let's pop into the secondhand shop." Lucie and Madame Blau behaved as though they had never met, but I had the feeling they recognized each other from the "old days." Madame Blau's family were Alsatian scrap metal merchants.

They hadn't been among those forcibly enlisted into the German army and who now lived scattered throughout the villages along the nearby river. Madame Blau had a limp and a slurred voice (*blau*, as it happens, means "drunk" in German), and a seemingly inexhaustible stock of goods. My mother was in her element. She loved to haggle. Eventually, delighted with her latest acquisition, she drove off in her 2CV with the children in tow. Madame Blau, dry-mouthed, watched us go, stuffed the banknotes into her apron pocket, and, with an alcoholic's suppressed wince, took a long swig of whisky straight from the bottle.

Why was she so well supplied with items to sell in this stony wine country? Where did all those little ivory opera glasses from the 1900 Paris World's Fair come from? All those albums filled with old postcards with affectionate messages, addressed to whom? Entire shelves of civil and military decorations of all kinds, with which insignia?

Years later I discovered that, as part of the *Möbel Aktion* (Furniture Operation), wagonloads of possessions stolen from Jews were transported from Paris to Germany and, along the way, to the town closest to Les Chomettes, where some items were taken off the transport to be stored in the local quarries. Two decades later, people began pilfering the goods from their hiding places and selling them off to dealers, who appeared to be largely unconcerned about their provenance. Who would recognize them down here anyway? Who was going to come and claim them? Most of the stuff was sold for next to nothing, since it had cost the sellers so little in the first place.

Lucie haggled fiercely, because she knew that Madame Blau had almost no costs associated with the goods she sold. Why should Blau be the only one to profit? This way the profits were shared around. Lucie was entitled to her share; she should be allowed to reap the rewards of her hard work too. It was thanks to her that Blau had all this. "You owe me!" she thought to herself. And it seemed that Madame Blau understood.

Another time she would suggest we "pop in" to visit the antiques dealer. This was a slightly more sustained variant of the first. The store, located in a small, quiet street in the neighboring town, was dimly lit and always open. While there were other local dealers, Monsieur Revel— pronounced clearly, with an emphasis on the second syllable—was, according to Lucie, the only proper professional. Monsieur Revel was Jewish, of course, but people pretended not to know, as if that allowed them to buy from him. He sold beautiful furniture and entire sets of valuable porcelain dinnerware. Where did he get it all from? Economical with words, he muttered a little and fell silent a lot. He made no effort to sell anything, even though he knew how rare and beautiful it all was. Lucie was not quite as at ease with him as with Madame Blau. She gave me an antique Sèvres dinner service with a turquoise-blue rim edged with gold. Suspicious of where it came from, I have never used it.

"Shall we go to the bookstore?" There were several bookstores in the nearby town, but we pretended there was only one. It was a little out of the way, near the so-called German villas, where Resistance fighters had been tortured.

In her thick gray serge skirt, with stringy hair knotted into a bun high on her head, and wearing a pair of black fingerless gloves, the bookseller looked like a witch. She was so unkempt, she could have been a female Céline. She sold banned books—by Céline, of course, and others—and was defensive and easily offended. However scary she seemed, standing there, one foot on each step, by the entrance to the store, shaking her fist at passersby, my mother always managed to placate her, and always intuited the right moment to leave. They seemed like old acquaintances.

She left with a pile of first editions as if she were carrying away her tithe. She had contributed to all this; it was only right she should be rewarded.

Another ritual was the visit to the local cemetery, which she presented to us as if it were a stroll or a ride on the merry-go-round: "Who's coming for a tour of the cemetery with me?" Friedrich wasn't even buried there, but Lucie acted as if she were visiting him. There was nothing to see, nothing to do with him anyway. Weeping, she walked me up and down the paths, stopping only to nod at various family plots. Ah, all the dead. Family. Family. Family. All the people who had known Friedrich were dead. And Friedrich himself was silent as a grave.

There was one grave that fascinated me. Right at the back of the cemetery, sitting on the bare earth, a simple pale pink wooden cradle, paint peeling off its bars. A white porcelain plaque surmounted by doves bore the words "To our beloved angel." Who was it? Someone's dead baby brother? Lucie nodded vaguely but was too overcome to answer. She was weeping for her past.

Calm at last, she began the slow descent from the cemetery on the hill to the village down below.

The house at Les Chomettes, in Lotharingia, was a conundrum. From the outside it looked like a small house in a Burgundy village on the side of a road with a tiled roof and stone walls. The entrance was down a side alley that led to the back of the house. It had been a gift from Lucie's father when she married Friedrich. Nothing was allowed to be changed, right down to the leaking roof still waiting to be repaired and the ancient electrical wires tightly wrapped in strips of fabric. There were closets filled with clothes and drawers stuffed with letters, identity documents, and wedding menus. Lucie smiled; it was like being back in 1941. Nothing could ever be changed, because Friedrich was coming back. The uncomfortable, higgledy-piggledy house with its multiple half levels was frozen in time, just like Miss Havisham's home. Nothing was missing, from the cotton percale curtains to the rustic furniture. In the dining room, chairs with heart-shaped backs (officially made in Franche-Comté, the region that borders Burgundy on one side and Alsace on the other, but in reality made by the German army as it advanced across occupied France) had been painted by Lucie with charming German-Alsatian floral motifs. A garland of brown ivy leaves, cut from wallpaper from another era, ran along the top of the wall. The floral frieze was neither Burgundian nor German; Lucie's decorative audacity was sometimes hard to pin down.

By the wall stood a rectangular table, a dark oak chest long enough for a child to lie down on, and a sideboard containing board games for us children to play after dinner. I was never sure what to make of *Clue*, devised in 1943, where the action takes place in a large country house and the player-detectives have to find out who killed whom, where, and how—Was it Colonel Mustard who murdered Miss Scarlett in the drawing room with a candlestick? There were more interesting games than *Monopoly*, in which, with money from who knows where, players buy up expensive property all over Paris. Lucie watched us play, a half smile on her face. There were games that were less mechanical than *Mille Bornes*, a game dating back to 1954, in which the players try to run away and avoid trouble by driving thousands of kilometers and setting obstacles to block their opponent.

The best game was one I invented, an updated version of *Happy Families*. In our family of Nazi sympathizers, I would pretend there was the mad scientist father, the collaborator mother, grandfather Pépé F., the morphine-addicted grandmother, the disturbed little girl, and the son who was in over his head. But nobody ever wanted to play with me.

The two top shelves of the sideboard contained a few interesting things, including large, brightly colored posters and pamphlets from another era. Lucie had a terrific collection, and she was very proud of it. Her favorite poster, which she would look at as if she were a connoisseur, had a vermilion-red background and was a denunciation of the Manouchian Resistance group. The poster showed small black-and-white identity photographs of the so-called terrorists. The pictures were captioned with hard-to-decipher names spelled with lots of consonants. One was easier to read than the rest: Manouchian. It reminded me of the word *Manouche*, which made me think of a gypsy passing through to pick cherries. According to the poster, these men were members of an "army of crime."

Lucie murmured, "It wouldn't have taken much for people to pity them, even though they were planning to blow everything up." I didn't understand, and my mother didn't explain. It would take me years to unravel the meaning of this notorious red poster.

One evening, around the All Saints' Day holiday, Lucie unfurled all the posters on the cherrywood dining room table. She stood pensively looking at them one last time, turned them over one by one, then rolled them up together. Wrapping her head in a large dark shawl like an old widow, she left the house and carried the bundle up the hill where she claimed the *Uhu* lived, the great horned owl. But it must have been an ordinary owl we heard at night, for the great horned owl, its wingspan two meters long, is the largest bird of prey in Europe, and no one had ever seen such a bird in the area. Did she mean the great horned owl or the Grand Duce? Lucie was always confusing her eagles.

Without a word, my mother threw the first posters into the tall flames of the bonfire she had prepared on a spur halfway up the hill and watched the fire burn. She didn't throw the next lot into the flames; she laid them down delicately, like an offering, poking the fire with a stick so the paper wouldn't fly away. The posters were damp and struggled to catch fire, but soon all that remained were embers. Lucie had burned the evidence.

All that was missing from this spectacular cremation, this dramatic, Nazi-style auto-da-fé, were banners and torches and an armed guard standing at attention. It was as if my mother were cremating Friedrich and her memories.

I was with her, the mute child, the only witness. I must have been about six. When it was over my mother made her way back down the cold November hillside, somber, head held high, in silence. She had reduced what she worshiped to ashes. From then on, the top two shelves of the sideboard remained empty, for nothing could replace what had been there.

It is difficult to believe after this that Lucie still believed in *als ob*, the magical "as if," the antidote to all pain. The analgesic was wearing off. She knew that she had lost, that Friedrich was never coming back. But she carried on pretending so that the fairy tales would live on, and because she owed it to him. When she said she was doing it for her children, she was lying to herself. Especially as there was another character on the wall above the fireplace in the dining room. It was a large red pastel drawing of an elderly man with a white moustache, in profile. When I asked who it was, my mother replied with a cagey smile that it had been done by a talented friend. But that didn't answer my question. It was a portrait of her grandfather, who looked like "someone." When the house was later burgled, the thieves didn't bother to take the picture, which still hangs on the wall. The portly, moustachioed man can sleep easy.

In the master bedroom, jagged-edged black-and-white photographs of Lucie when she was young, blond, and beautiful were pinned to the walls. In some of them part of the image is obscured, so that the person she is smiling at cannot be seen. Her new husband had to put up with it. It was he who placed an enamel plaque on Friedrich's grave in Normandy, with his first and last names, the year of his birth, and the year of his death.

In the barn, Friedrich's sealskins and mountaineering gear were lined up along the wall. The camping kit, with its scratched bowls, was a little tarnished, but sports and outdoor activities were going to be taken up again. At least Lucie hadn't burned all this. Upstairs, dust gathered on the 1943 ten-volume edition of Masson's anatomical pathology (the volume entitled *Urogenital Apparatus* bears the marks of curious little fingers) alongside some rusty dissecting equipment, and a razor-sharp scalpel. My brother still uses the curved dissecting scissors as magnificent nail scissors. The darkroom materials are also still in use. And Friedrich is still there, "just over the way."

Except there is no transcendence at Les Chomettes. Nazis, and true Burgundians, are not Christian.

But the temple and its high priestess needed servants of memory from beyond the family circle. Those who knew Friedrich were asked to contribute, in a kind of deal. *You keep his memory alive, and I will support you.* Lucie showed great devotion to the childhood friends she put to work for her.

A large half-moon sofa covered in an electric blue synthetic from the fabric maker Nobilis with a ghastly moiré geometric pattern was stranded on an upper floor. Nobody ever sat on it. Who would want to, if not Friedrich's ghost?

In exchange, the friends proved their loyalty, repeating their lines as flawlessly as a Greek chorus. A passing allusion or discreet reminiscence of happy times was enough. "*Lu-cie!* What a time it was! Oh, did we know how to have fun." They knew how to flatter their friend, noting with a touch of jealousy how handsome her "boyfriend" Charles was. He was handsome, her second husband, though there was nothing boyish about him.

On one or two occasions, one or another of the friends forgot that time had also passed for her, and she flagrantly began a relationship with one of the children's teenage friends. The generation gap between the charming, shy young man and his well-preserved paramour seemed not to bother anyone. Lucie didn't interfere.

Back in Paris, life was not as much fun as it had been. Lucie had lost her bearings. She was renting an apartment that had never been lived in by Friedrich, and she felt suffocated.

She read all the time, books and far-right magazines like Le *Spectacle du monde* and *Valeurs actuelles*. Some of the writers were familiar names from the past, such as Pierre Gaxotte and Jacques Benoist-Méchin. Their style had become more measured, but the substance had not changed.

Lucie resumed her dealing. At the monthly municipal credit auctions, she bought jewelry by weight or in lots to restock her sister's antique store. These were items that had been pawned by people in need of cash that would be sold, if the money was not repaid, after one year and one day. Lucie was reimbursed the purchase price by her sister, who then sold the goods on at a higher price. A family affair. It reminded her of the time when vast quantities of jewelry, paintings, and furniture were used as security.

She had a good eye and could tell when a piece of jewelry was pure gold or if it was gold-plated copper, tarted up, "pomponné." Gold and *pomponne*. Real and fake. The genuine and the ersatz. Like substitute sweetener, which looks like sugar, but isn't. Ersatz sugar. Ersatz gold. *Als ob*.

Which laws are substitutes for other laws? All so confusing, but I couldn't let it go. There were laws, and there was the Law.

And why such loyalty to a dead husband?

We had regular family discussions about poison and toxic gases. Lucie seemed to know all about them. ("Right, Maman? It's true, no?") She taught us about the properties of prussic acid, discovered, of course, in Prussia, and found in minute quantities in cherry pits (we children peered suspiciously at the familiar fruit). Strychnine was touted as the miracle poison, promising instant death (we were a little taken aback by this). A cyanide capsule can be hidden in the hollow of a molar. My mother's expression grew avid, her eyes bright. This was the ultimate.

What a lighthearted way to conjure up death! Although she never mentioned it, Lucie must have known the fate of many of the Nazi dignitaries. Göring. Himmler. It was the Third Reich, it was only going to end badly, and yet, for most of them, it was unembodied, a theoretical death. Göring's suicide looks strange in the newspaper image, one eye still half-open.

Lucie and Friedrich had built up a big collection of insecticide bombs. The number one most important thing was the word *bombs*, followed by the fact that they could kill. Some were for flying insects (to prevent air attacks) and some for crawling insects (to prevent ground attacks). Their favorite brand was German, of course, and it made a wide range of products. Lucie couldn't remember whether her favorite day cream, in its metallic blue tin, was from this brand or another one. She always got them mixed up. Her favorite German drug company didn't make everything, after all.

She rarely socialized in the milieu of her second husband and even more rarely accompanied him on his business trips, although she did in 1971, when he was invited by the Shah of Iran to the 2,500th anniversary of the founding of the Persian Empire. She adored the lavish ceremonies. It reminded her that the Reich had been meant to last a thousand years. Lucie wasn't bothered by Charles's dealings with tyrants: She enjoyed chatting with them, especially the young colonel Gaddafi, for whom she held an undisguised admiration: so handsome, such poise! Maybe he reminded her of Il Duce. At times like this, her husband was worth the bother.

When it came to his colleagues' wives, however, Lucie felt a tinge of disdain. They were so gauche and silly and narrow-minded. One evening, at a cocktail party with her husband, Lucie bumped into an old classmate, Bianca. Both Bianca's surname and her waistline had changed since school, but the two recognized each other at once. Bianca had married a boring academic—a Jew, of course—which Lucie immediately translated in her mind as "He seems terribly intelligent." It felt awkward to hark back to their school days. Back in 1938, when they were seventeen and at the same Parisian lycée, Bianca had had a relationship with their philosophy teacher, Simone de Beauvoir, whom Lucie loved for her feminist and free spirit. But it wasn't the kind of thing to bring up at an elegant soiree. As the two couples exchanged lighthearted conversation, Lucie couldn't get it out of her head: Bianca had survived. She must have gone into hiding. Jewish girls were easy to spot, especially this one, with her English governess and chauffeur-driven car to ferry her to school.

She had escaped the camps.

Clearly their experiences during the Occupation had been very different. Bianca did not mention the people she had lost, her uncle and aunt, the parents of Georges Perec, who was adopted in 1945, aged nine, by Bianca's parents. But Lucie was not interested anyway. The enemies remained the same.

Lucie got older, the children grew up, and the years that passed didn't show on her.

She remained obsessed with the collaboration. She was an ambassador for a lost cause, an empress without an empire, a Gaul without a district, made for Lotharingia. You had to understand the way she used figures of speech, instinctively, so as not to name it: analogy, transposition, metaphor, displacement, syllepsis, metonymy, synecdoche. But she did talk about it. All the time. It was all she ever talked about, while never overtly mentioning it.

Fortunately, there was *als ob*.

7

AFTER SO MUCH EXCITEMENT and misbehavior during the Occupation, the next six decades seemed flat, dull, and monotonous. The clan carried on their lives in a state of continuity, barely distracted by the raised voices of their various disputes. They had lived so intensely, and they continued to dwell on it all.

The gynaeceum hewed to the road map drawn up by Lucie, who, a consummate strategist, succeeded in fading into the background for the rest of her life. You cannot both be and have been. Most of the clan lived on to a great old age, watching one another intently, always on the lookout for the slightest sign of weakness.

They died without ever having spoken, leaving everything as it was, unresolved.

Since time stood still for all of them, they remained, in a way, the same age they had been during the Occupation. Simultaneously old and young, they reinforced this image of themselves by holding up a distorting mirror to one another.

Aunt Zizi grew mournful and kept fit with gymnastic exercises, to the detriment of her aching joints, while Lucie, a tenacious old-young woman, did everything she could to ignore the fact that her arteries and bones were not keeping up; Rafi-the-Magnificent remained in spirit an eternally adventurous young man, trying to keep the weight off with the help of a masseur and regular physical training. My grandmother Herminette, stuck in her overheated apartment, drifted in and out of her morphine stupor until she forgot who she was, while my grandfather lay in bed counting out gold napoleons in his rasping voice, declaring himself at the ready to resume fighting the eternal enemies of France.

My grandfather died first, weakened by too many good meals with his old fascist friends, hunting buddies, and regimental comrades. He caught a cold and that was it. While her father faded away in the hospital, Lucie was away with Charles on a business trip in America.

The widowed Herminette continued injecting herself with morphine for several more years until she too died in the hospital. Her daughter Zizi moved out of her apartment and into her mother's.

Raphaël lived on for another twenty years until in his nineties he became aphasic. Two weeks before his death he was still holding forth with great dignity. As he began showing signs of decline, Aunt Zizi tried to take his beloved chaise longue, what he always called his whore's bed, on the pretext that she was going to get it restored, but he shook his head vehemently, a sad expression on his face. Lucie had gradually been emptying his bank accounts with, I hope, his conscious consent.

Ten years later, at the turn of the twenty-first century, Lucie had a heart attack at home and died, taking her secrets with her. Thirty seconds of pain for a death foretold, sudden, swift, and violent. "It hurts, I'm going to die," she said simply, as her hand loosened. It was a spirited exit, as they say in the theater, an expression I think she would have liked. A dignified end for a strong-willed woman. She could not have borne being sick or dependent on anyone. "You'll see all that when I'm dead," she used to say enigmatically. Her children saw. She had given up the shares that were rightfully hers, to the detriment of her children. The house at Les Chomettes went to her son Félix—that is, to Friedrich—and I am not sure that was a gift.

I breathed a discreet sigh of relief. At last, I could begin to live my life freely. The few pieces of furniture Lucie had given to me during her lifetime were a source of curiosity, particularly a large two-way mirror in a magnificent antique frame. During the Occupation, this type of mirror was opportunely transformed and used in Gestapo interrogations. The accused would stand behind the glass, in which he thought he could see only himself reflected. *Do you know this man?*

The mirror had been salvaged from a brothel that had been closed down by the Germans, where clients could peer undisturbed through the mirror and choose whom they desired to satisfy their fantasies.

Where did Lucie get it from? It was "in the cellar," of course. But whose cellar?

Today, the large frame, adorned by two winged sphinxes with lions' paws and women's busts under the auspices of Aspasia, like an ancient Greek courtesan, surrounds a new mirror, this time made of ordinary silvered glass, without a past. An expert established that at some point a Renaissance painting from a Florentine palazzo had been removed and replaced with a mirror. The frame was black with smoke and the restoration was slow. Not even an expert could tell what this mirror has seen, and that is a good thing.

I have never been able to connect this mirror with any episode in Lucie's life. Was she an escort for U.S. Army officers before her exfiltration? Or was it the fulfilment of some dark fantasy? Is there a part of her life that remains in shadow, a black hole I know nothing about? All I can say is that I inherited a large brothel mirror from my mother.

Aunt Zizi did not live much longer after her sister died. She had lost her West and her East. "*But Lu-cie?*" A stroke rendered her speech incomprehensible, and her cropped black hair turned white. No one recognized the woman who had once had the energy of a jumping jack. And despite owning several properties all over France, she ended her life in a retirement home.

Now a widower, my father gradually began to lose his marbles. After decades of consuming a powerful antipsychotic known as a chemical straitjacket, usually given to the mentally ill to help them sleep, which he took with benzodiazepines as if he were swallowing a couple of aspirin and some vitamin C, he ended up confusing francs and euros, driving around roundabouts the wrong way, and trying to seduce anything in a skirt. He remained living at home with full-time help for thirteen years. He died when he was almost ninety-nine, having forgotten everything, even the names of his children. But he never forgot the name of his wife, Lucie. He had only one wish: to be laid to rest beside her. And so he was.

All Lucie's childhood friends, the Greek chorus, lived to be a hundred, or nearly. Pierrette, Josette, Suzette, Zouzou, face-lifted, massaged, manicured, coiffed, died within a few months of one another, as if they had been keeping one another alive. One of the friends, a childless widow, bequeathed a magnificent collection of revolutionary-era plates to the museum in the next town. A strange bequest from a former good-time girl whose main topics of conversation had always been epilation and self-tanning.

Uncle Gaston, the former editorial director of the mass circulation collaborationist newspaper, died relatively young, at sixty-five, as if he no longer considered it worth living if it meant being forced to witness the triumph of his great rival and lifelong enemy Lazareff. Ah, that Lazarus. His God must have helped him.

And then there were the Henriots. The clan seemed to make every effort to insinuate that they were related to Philippe, the great propagandist; anything that might connect us to him was simultaneously emphasized and carefully dismissed. We never drank Bordeaux, which might have put us in mind of the Gironde, where the great man was buried, nor did we dare take to our lips a glass of the ill-fated Henriot Champagne. Fortunately, his butterfly collection had been exiled to a museum in Karlsruhe, Germany. Somewhere, his ghost was still flitting around.

Lucie continued to regularly visit Friedrich's burial site in a remote corner of Normandy. She stood and wept by his grave while Charles stood a short distance behind her and we children didn't know what to do with ourselves in the face of such maternal despair. She kept extending the lease on the plot, despite repeated requests from Friedrich's family to have his body transferred to the family vault in Haute-Alsace. She did not want him to leave the cemetery, as if that would somehow displace her grief.

Eventually the lease expired, for Lucie was no longer around to extend it. Friedrich's remains would be dug up and buried in a common grave. What ought we to do?

My brother and I, Friedrich's "children," had a conflict of loyalties. Of course, we were not his children, but he had been a huge part of our childhood and our mother's life. He had been such a presence in our father's life too that our father even requested that after he died the words "To she who was unfaithful" be inscribed in Latin on his wife's tombstone. In his will he slightly modified the phrase, which was still to be inscribed in Latin: "To she who was unfaithful just once."

We did not carry out his wishes. At least not literally, but we did later, in a different way, because eventually we came to understand what he meant. Our father knew that Lucie had only ever loved one man, Friedrich. She had cheated on Charles only once, though it lasted her whole marriage, and was always with the same man. Or the memory of the same man.

We decided to lay Lucie and Friedrich to rest together. It was such a beautiful love story. A Nazi tale, to be sure, but a love story nonetheless. They would be in the company of the faithful Charles, who had always insisted that you cannot be jealous of a dead man, hinting perhaps at how much he had suffered. We sought various bureaucratic authorizations and approached Friedrich's sole heir for his permission. The body was exhumed from the small cemetery in Le Plessis, Normandy. Almost eighty years after his death, there was very little left. His remains were placed in a small black box, which travelled at low speed in a hearse halfway across France to Lotharingia. There was no torch-lit procession. Friedrich was reburied in the cemetery at Les Chomettes, next to Lucie, who lies next to Charles. We gave a brief eulogy and reaffixed the funeral plaque.

And so we made official, albeit not in Latin, what our father had requested be chiseled on her gravestone after his death: our mother had loved another man, despite everything.

Though it would probably have been better to let the dead bury the dead so that we could begin to exhume our lost illusions, we chose to lay them to rest together, in a tomb for three. It is all we have managed to salvage from the story.

Friedrich, who might have become a kind of Mengele if he had lived, was laid to rest in a proper grave alongside his beloved Lucie.

By burying the assigned father alongside the father who had abdicated his responsibilities and the mother who was a crazed fanatic, we have given them each their place. Friedrich and Lucie, like recumbent effigies in a cathedral, have found their true position as a couple on the family tree, while

Charles, with whom Lucie lived the longest, is the third, like a faithful lion watching over and sometimes warming the feet of their reclining figures.

But the main thing is that, by burying Friedrich in the family plot, we have buried him, at last, once and for all. We have rid ourselves of him; it is we who have laid him to rest and not death that has taken him.

Here lies Friedrich, Gauleiter of Lotharingia, henceforth buried in his rightful place.

Here lies Lucie and here lies Charles. Spirits flit around my mother, spirits possessed by demons, as she liked to say, like guardian angels of evil. The great-uncles, the real ones, the half ones, the fake ones, the almost-related ones. Laughing their heads off.

My own laughter is still a little bitter.